COULD IT BE YOU?

LOVE IN DUNES BAY

BOOK THREE

LYNN CRANDALL

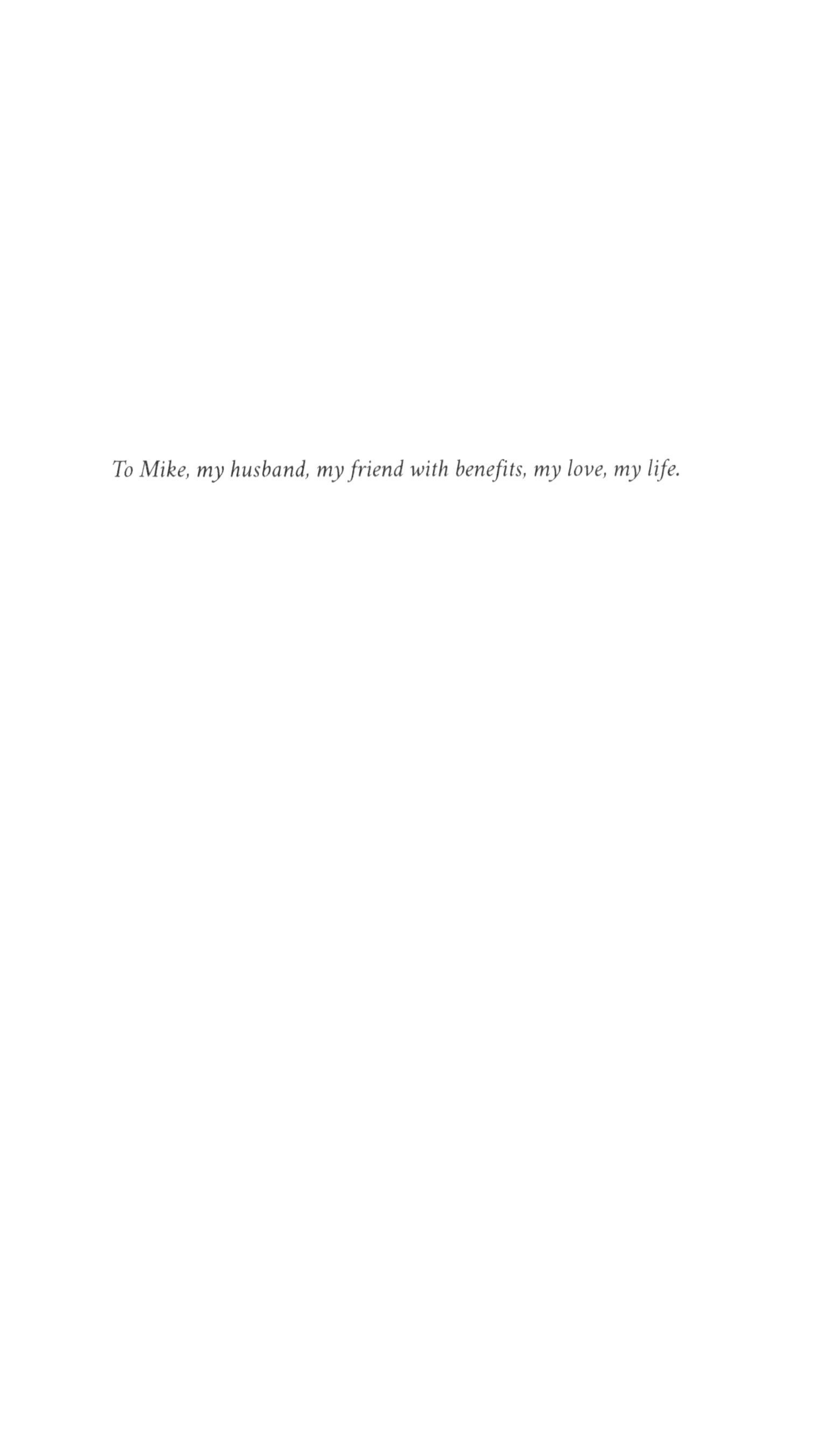

To Mike, my husband, my friend with benefits, my love, my life.

From The Author

It has been a pleasure to write the Love in Dunes Bay series. Each book explores life on the beach of a large inland lake for each of the main characters. The stories are set in a fictitious town on the very real Lake Michigan for a reason: I love the lake. I grew up in Michigan and spent many hours on Lake Michigan beaches. It's a lifestyle that can't be duplicated.

The themes explored in the series books include family, found family, and romance. Each book also explores healing from wounds inflicted in the past and how these wounds if left undiscovered can direct the present and the future. For characters, leaving the false beliefs and unhealed wounds is challenging and scary. To face them, it takes courage and support and the decision to take a risk in order to find peace and true love.

I hope you enjoy reading Could It Be You? and the closure it gives to the series. Thank you for your support

Hugs,
    Lynn Crandall

CHAPTER 1

Jasper Steele grabbed his medic kit and jumped out the back doors of the ambulance. "Let's go, Tavis!" he said, and took off toward a man stretched out on the ground beside a car, blood pooling all around his head.

He dropped to his knees and checked for a pulse, tuning out everything but the possibility of a slight beat of the man's heart.

"I told you the man is dead," said the officer standing off to the side. "A gunshot to the back of the head will do that to you."

The Dunes Bay police officer on the scene had filled in Jasper and Tavis when they arrived: Patient deceased; probable cause—gunshot. But Jasper had a duty to confirm the cop's *diagnosis*.

"What's his name?" Jasper preferred to interact personally with patients. Using a name helped make a connection.

The officer looked at the ID in his hand. "His drivers' license says Devin Raye."

A shock wave flew through Jasper. Oh my god. This guy was Cherish's would-be husband. He stared at the man's face, wondering if Cherish ever thought about the man she almost married a little over a year ago. Or did marrying his big brother Grayson erase everything about her awful relationship with Devin?

He checked his watch and noted it was eleven in the morning. He had to let her know. But right now he couldn't. The man on the ground was Jasper's priority and he looked rough, with blood everywhere and bruised and swollen eyes. Blood from the bullet wound pooled around his head and dampened his dark hair. Jasper's stomach tightened and he checked again for signs of life.

"Tavis, he has a pulse and he's breathing but they're both faint," Jasper shouted to his partner still at the rig. Both of them were working a partial shift for two other members of the team who needed personal time. Lucky for him, he'd gotten some sleep last night. Though he had worked his usual six to six shift, Jasper's mind and body perched on alert.

After five years as an EMT with the city of Dunes Bay Emergency Services, Jasper was still sensitive to the results of violence, but everything in him determined to save Devin, despite what he'd done, just as he would with any other patient. It's what he did.

"I'll give him a bolus of fluids to help boost his blood pressure and heart rate," Tavis added, "and then check his vitals."

"I'll administer oxygen." Jasper fitted an oxygen mask over the patient's nose and mouth. "A bullet wound in his head, and bruising of the face and neck. Defensive wounds on his hands. He must have put up a fight before losing consciousness."

"He really got a beating. I bet whoever attacked him didn't realize he wasn't dead when they left the scene." Tavis pushed fluids through the IV. "This is going to help you feel better, guy."

"Hey, Devin. Stay with me." Jasper put his hand on the man's shoulder. "We're taking care of you, but I need you to stay with us."

Tavis listened to Devin's heart and checked his blood pressure again. "His pulse is stronger. His blood pressure is sixty-six over forty."

Jasper rolled his eyes. That was not good. "Okay, let's bring out the stretcher and get him to the ER."

The siren from a police cruiser drew louder and Jasper sighed. They didn't need more cops.

Two minutes later, the cruiser drove up, followed by a dark blue Volkswagen Beetle. Jasper exchanged a glance with Tavis.

Tavis lifted his brows. "Detectives."

Jasper shrugged. "Of course. Suspicious circumstances like this are their territory."

Two detectives opened the door on each car. Jasper nodded at one of them. He knew all the cops in Dunes Bay, including Jordan Graves. The one from the VW, a woman, walked closer. She marched toward him as though on a mission.

"Jasper," Tavis said. "Are we still going to load up?" He stared at the woman.

"Yeah, we're running fast on this one." Jasper dismissed the approaching detective and jumped up into the back of the rig to help Tavis pull out the stretcher and run it to the patient.

Seconds later, they dropped it to the ground and secured the patient's head with a neck brace.

"On two," Jasper said, bent over the man on the ground. "One, two!"

Gently, Jasper placed the man's head and shoulders on the stretcher at the same time Tavis lifted his legs. Swiftly, they loaded him into the bus. They each took their place—Tavis at the wheel and Jasper in back with the patient."

The officer started to close the back doors but the female detective stopped him.

"Excuse me. I'll take over, officer," she said with a dismissive wave of her hand.

"Sure thing." Officer Graves, along with the others checking the scene, backed away.

She turned her gaze on Jasper. "What's your name?"

He sighed. "Jasper. We have a man close to death, Detective, so if you'll pardon me, I'm going to follow protocol, which does not allow extra time to chat."

"I'm working on a case this murder might be connected to. Could we talk briefly?"

Her eyes were dark and glistening. She shot an earnest look at him. He could have caved right then.

In his hesitation, the woman spoke up. "Can't we be professional and talk just for a minute? I need to know details about the crime scene or the suspects who murdered him are going to get away."

Her expression was stern, but he had his priorities. "Don't say murdered. This man is alive. And he has a name, Devin Raye. What's your name?" Jasper asked.

"Dobson Maria Perez Ramirez. I'm a detective with Dunes Bay PD."

"Yeah, I got that."

This was a ridiculous waste of time and so *not* typical. Maybe she was new. He'd never seen her before, so he repressed an urge to slam the doors in her face and take off. "I can talk with you at the hospital. We have to go."

"Just one question. You say he's alive, but how could he not be dead after being shot in the head?" She pursed her lips.

Jasper could see the wheels in her head moving. Though annoying, her question was sincere. "The scalp stretches. If the bullet hits just right, the scalp can slow down its momentum and prevent it from penetrating dangerously close to the brain."

"So he got lucky," she said.

"Yeah." He pulled the doors closed and Tavis turned on the siren. Seconds later they were streaming down the road to the hospital.

DOBSON WATCHED the ambulance tear away and clenched her teeth. A sliver of shame gnawed at her gut for delaying their run to the hospital. Jasper had accused her of breaking protocol. Yes, she was new on the Dunes Bay force, but it made her cringe to think she'd already made a mistake. She wasn't new to police work. She'd been so eager, that's all.

"I'm going to stick around and look over the scene," said Officer Graves. "Forensics should be here any minute."

A nano second of a thought perked her up. "Yeah, a phone would be nice, but check the roadside for anything, Jordan," she said. Jordan was one of the few officers she'd met at DBPD. "Footprints, cigarettes, tire tracks, anything we could use for an ID. I'm going to follow the ambulance."

Behind her back as she walked to her car she heard Jordan and the other officers scruffing through the weeds near the edge of the road, which told her they didn't need babysitting.

She slid behind the wheel and drove onto the road. Nature surrounded her in rolling hills and thick groves of trees. While it all passed by outside the car windows, her brain ran possibilities. The moment Jasper said the victim's name, her insides clenched. Working on a task force with the FBI, she'd seen his name come up in her investigation into the Esposito crime organization. She'd been waiting for a return call from Devin so they could set up a time for an interview.

Dobson let out a long breath, hoping the medic, Jasper, knew what he was talking about. The odds of surviving a bullet were not in the victim's favor. She mentally crossed her fingers that Devin would make it.

She blew some strands of hair out of her face, frustration burning in her chest. Two weeks in Dunes Bay and she still didn't have much of a case against the infamous Espositos. One of the most dangerous crime organizations in the country, they were skilled at evading prosecution. Things she discovered during her research so far disgusted her. They didn't do their own dirty work; they got other people to do it. People like Adrian and Emma Moss.

Trees and occasional traffic blurred by her as impatience pressed the gas pedal down. She had been counting on getting a trove of info from Devin and his devices, but she couldn't wait for him to recover. She might be down but she was not out. She wasn't ever going to be the undermined and dismissed woman she had been in the Chicago Police Department. That was a promise she made to herself when she put all that Chicago stuff behind her and transferred to Dunes Bay. She'd been watching the jobs board for a while when an opening in the PD here caught her eye. When she got the job offer, Dobson didn't hesitate to accept it. It took her a matter of days to make arrangements for her mother to move with her. Never would she ever leave her mom behind.

No. This new start would work out for both of them. Her mom had always been there, kept her alive practically when her father was killed on the street. Sadness suddenly ached in her chest, remembering her loss at eight years old.

A shake of her head and Dobson shifted back to the case at hand and the possible loss of a primary witness. The one she'd failed to keep safe. "Oh gosh," she muttered. Had she made another unforgivable mistake in judgement?

"No, don't do that to yourself, Dobson," she said, gathering her courage. "Don't tear yourself down because that won't help anything."

Back in her office, she put her mind to the piles of evidence waiting in her office. Among the files was information the Mosses had given her about Teddy, the big man in the Esposito crime organization. After years of laundering money for him and doing other illegal things through their law firm, they'd turned state's witnesses and provided key information. Officers in the organized crime department at DBPD had pressured them before she'd arrived, using threats and promises of jail time. Her MO took a softer angle and offered a way out of a lifestyle that had taken them down like quicksand. They'd been adamant their two daughters had never been involved, and quite stubborn about their own culpability. Kicking and hollering they came around and now had her gratitude for their cooperation.

She checked the time. Eight-thirty in the morning. The drive to the hospital from the outskirts of Dunes Bay would take about fifteen minutes more, she predicted. It took all of her patience not to floor it.

CHAPTER 2

The ER doors parted and Dobson strode in, perusing the waiting room. A sense of urgency mingled with the sound of soft crying from children on their mothers' laps swept over her. The room buzzed with tension. She spotted a security guard and showed him her badge, and he directed her to the head doctor, who eyed her and her badge.

"I see," she said, and handed back Dobson's badge. "I'm Doctor Hannah Smith. How can I help you, Detective?

"I'm checking on a patient I need to talk to about his accident. He probably just arrived. He'd suffered a bullet in his head. Do you know if he survived?" Dobson tapped her foot on the shiny tile floor.

"Hmm, it's too soon to say. The ambulance arrived about ten minutes ago. I'm sorry, the patient went right into surgery. He's likely still there. It's on the fourth floor. Look for a nurse at the nurses' station. One of them can give you updated information."

Before she could ask anything more, a nurse called for Dr. Smith and she hurried to a patient across the room, which was okay because Dobson needed to get to the surgical floor.

At the elevator, she pressed the button for the fourth floor and rode with a young man and woman. They got off at the third floor and she blew out a breath. Suspicion automatically rose in her gut, knowing the Espositos had their fingers on pulse points of everything and probably knew Devin hadn't died immediately. They would want to fix that.

She strolled toward the nurses' station, her eyes taking in the surroundings, but she didn't see anything amiss. She got to the counter and cleared her throat, just to interrupt all the activity. One nurse held her hand over the phone receiver.

"Can I help you?" she asked.

Dobson popped out her badge again and began to speak, but the nurse started talking on the phone again. She counted the sticky notes around the desk. *One, two, three, four, fi...*

"I'm sorry," the nurse said while she hung up the phone. "You were saying?"

"I'm Detective Ramirez. Could you tell me the condition of a man brought to surgery from the ER? Patient name is Devin Raye."

The nurse looked through the computer and quickly answered the question.

"Mr. Raye is presently in surgery, probably will be for maybe two hours."

Dobson's eyes closed briefly. *He wasn't dead yet.*

"You could get something to eat in the cafeteria if you're hungry," the nurse suggested, and pointed across the hall. The nurse spoke her words in a clipped tone to match the ongoing bustle around her. "Or wait in the waiting room and I'll notify you of any changes if they occur."

"Thank you. I'll just wait over there."

Her shoes clicked as she walked to the waiting room a few yards from the nursing station. Her eyes darted around the room, searching for anyone suspicious. Nope. It was just her suspicious mind, not gut instinct. She let out a breath and took a lone seat where she would have a hint of privacy.

Her gaze flitted to the magazines piled on a small nearby table but decided against reading one of them. *Two hours? What was I thinking? I can't sit here for two hours.*

She walked over to the wall of windows and scanned the scene below. The sun was high in the afternoon sky. Perfect day to spend at the beach, she thought. From her fourth floor vantage point she could see doctors parking in their designated area and walking toward the building. An ambulance charged up the road and swerved into the driveway to the emergency entrance.

The emergency entrance where her car still sat.

"Dang it," she exclaimed. How could she have forgotten? She raced to the elevators and pressed the ground floor button. What seemed like way too many minutes later, she charged out the main door and ran to her car.

Breathing heavily, she put her hand on the driver's door almost at the same time a security guard stepped up.

"Officer," she gasped. "I'm so sorry for leaving my car unattended."

He glared at her through his dark sunglasses. Or at least she imagined he did. She couldn't actually see his eyes.

The guard shoved his cellphone into his pocket. "I was just about to call for a tow."

"I had to get to an injured person quickly."

"Hey, Oscar. How's your day going?"

She knew that voice. Dobson twisted her head around to see Jasper the EMT toward her. Her heart thrummed in her chest. What did he want?

"Hey, Jas. I'm good. Just helping this woman with her car." The guard smiled at Jasper.

"Oh, helping?" Jasper winked at her. "This is Detective Dobson Ramirez. Are you sure you need to *help* her?" He made air quotes around the word help and grinned at the guard.

"I was just apologizing to him." Dobson pulled at the edge of her suit coat.

"Miss, just because I'm in a good mood, thanks to Jas here, I'm going to warn you not to leave your car here again and let you move it to an appropriate parking space." The security guard looked over the edge of his dark glasses. "You do understand, don't you?"

She quickly pulled out her keys from her pants pocket. "Yes, I'm moving it right now. Thank you."

"Just doing my job. Have a good afternoon."

The guard walked inside, leaving Dobson trembling slightly. "Whew, that was close."

"Aww, Oscar is a good guy. He understood."

"I'm so stupid. I just ran inside and forgot about my car." Dobson wanted to crawl inside her car and flee the scene. Her mistakes in Dunes Bay were piling up.

"If forgetting is the definition of stupid then I must be a bonehead. I forget things all the time. It's stress induced." He waved his hand dismissively. "Nothing to worry about."

She rolled her eyes. "Whatever." It would take more than his assurance to quiet the voice in her head always ready to remind her of her poor judgment.

"It's getting close to noon. Would you want to go to lunch with me? I know a great lunch counter and we could discuss Mr. Raye."

Jasper's crystal blue eyes met hers head on. She couldn't escape his sincerity.

"Can I get a rain check?" Dobson lowered her gaze. "I left the surgical floor just to move my car. I need to focus on work. I can do that best by waiting on the fourth floor for Mr. Raye to go into recovery."

"If he goes into recovery," Jasper inserted.

A lump formed in her throat. "Whichever way it goes, I want to be there."

"I understand. I could get a nurse on the surgical floor to call me when he comes out."

"You're persistent. But I do need to stay focused, here." She pointed to the towering hospital building. "Thank you for the offer." Her face flushed, and she ducked in behind the wheel.

He stood with his hand on the door for another few seconds. "Okay, another time, then." He shrugged while closing the door and strolled away. She stared, transfixed by his large shoulders and easy walking pace.

Snap out of it. Slowly she drove to a parking space and turned off the car. She envied Jasper's laid back attitude. Something in her told her she was too constrained, too determined to keep people away, too afraid of rejection. Her heart longed to relax and let go of the past. Let. Go. Of. The. Past.

Tears welled in her eyes and she brushed them away, disgusted. She knew her heart wasn't in control, her wounds were.

* * *

AT NOON, his overtime was over. Jasper clocked out at the house, then drove to the hospital. How could he stop himself? Yes, Dobson had been annoying. But her attitude about the crime scene— expecting to get what she wanted and taking over—was not far from that of many detectives he'd had dealings with. Usually he just ignored them. But with her it was different. He wanted to help her. And, he wanted to know why. Why did the need to help tug at him so hard?

He reached the elevator inside the hospital and took it to the fourth floor. Briskly, he walked to the nursing station and gestured to one of the nurses he knew. She frowned, but came to the counter.

"What," she asked, all matter of fact.

"Whoa, that wasn't friendly." Jasper frowned.

"C'mon, Jasper. Cut me some slack." Her shoulders sank. "Sorry, it's been a hectic morning. Unless you've got a cup of Coffee Easy coffee for me, get to the point."

"Got it, Krista. I need an update on a patient I brought in to the ER. He went into surgery and—"

"Name?" she asked without looking up from her computer screen.

"Devin Raye."

"He's still in surgery. Then he'll go to recovery, so that's it." She looked up with tired eyes and smiled.

"Meaning he's not up for visitors for several hours, but at least he's alive." Jasper gave her a wide smile.

"Yes, that is his status. He probably won't have visitors today, if that's what you're thinking. If all goes well, he'll go to the ICU." Krista pushed away from her desk. "Sorry for being short." She smiled again.

"I understand. I appreciate the update," Jasper said, drumming his hands in a short beat on the counter. "I'll get out of your way."

She turned away from him and plunged into her work. Hmm… Dobson said she'd wait for Devin to wake up, but that's not going to happen, it's going to take a while, if it even happens. He followed the signs to the waiting room, and immediately saw her shiny dark hair standing out in the roomful of others.

He strolled to her, hardening to her anger, so hopefully they could be civil to each other this time.

"Mind if I sit here?" he asked her, gesturing to the open seat beside her. "I come in peace."

"Sure." She chewed on her lower lip.

He nodded, noting her nervousness, and slid into the chair. "I talked with a nurse and she told me it will be awhile, as in days, before you'd be able to talk with Devin."

She turned abruptly to face him. "Days! Oh crap. I wish the nurses would have told me," she said. "They simply blew me off."

"Hold on. It's been a hectic day for them. Don't take it personally. It's possible Devin's status changed during surgery."

He watched her expression drop and she averted her eyes. He didn't blame her for getting upset. Regardless of the jokes, cops had plenty more to do than just sit around and nap or eat doughnuts.

Dobson shoved her notebook into her purse and got up. Her phone rang and she pulled it out of her pocket. "Hello? Hello? Who is this?"

Her face blanched, and she hung up, her eyes wide. Fumbling around with her phone, she looked disoriented, troubled.

"Is there a problem?" Jasper asked.

"No, that was just a crank call. I've been getting them lately."

"Do you know who was on the other end?"

She gave a sharp laugh. "Pick a name."

"What?"

"Nothing." She knitted her brow. "Thank you for letting me know about Devin. I'll see you around, probably."

"No problem." He ground his teeth and let her go, waiting until she'd made it to the elevator to give her space to gain composure. The doors opened and she gave her hair a flip, then walked inside.

Wow, he thought to himself. She's a powder keg. Why? Obviously, she had experience in her field and skills to get her job done. She wouldn't be at DBPD if that weren't so. Parts of him wanted to run after her and tell her she was fine. Sure she'd screwed up, but so what? Everybody does.

No, that was his pattern. Always making sure people were okay, especially his mother and father, and now that he was thirty years old, he was paying the price for taking care of others. He was invisible and it felt like crap.

Dobson's annoyance was not his problem, and besides, *he* was annoyed with *her*. He shook his head to clear it.

He could dismiss her. But her agitation sparked his curiosity. And that was worth pursuing. If he were honest with himself, he had been a player, dating women casually and wanting fun, no strings attached. But Dobson, with her quick temper was potentially different, interesting. What was behind her agitation?

He jumped up and took the stairs to the first floor, his heart thudding hard in his chest. He'd probably miss her but he was hoping he wouldn't, as he shoved through the first floor door and scanned the area.

There she was across the large lobby and nearly to the door outside. He sped to her, weaving through the crowd.

"Dobson, stop," he called.

She looked up, as though she'd heard him but not certain.

Just then, he put his hand on her shoulder from behind and she turned her dark eyes on him. "Phew, I almost didn't make it."

"Make what?"

"Umm, well." Now that Jasper was here he was befuddled.

"Yes?" Dobson tilted her head, as though trying to understand him.

Spit it out, man! "I just wanted to see if you're all right."

"Of course. Why wouldn't I be?"

Yes, why wouldn't she be? "Because you can't interview the patient for a while, or maybe ever. I think the question sounded more sane in my head." Heat spread to his cheeks. "I can see you're fine, so," Jasper took two steps back. "I'll just see you around."

"Stop." Dobson put her hand to his arm. "I don't know why you think I can't handle a little set back, but it's sweet that you cared."

What? She thinks I care. He bit his tongue. He wanted to deny her statement. He wanted to straighten her out. But everything was getting all turned around and upside down, so he just smiled.

"I can handle it, you know. I can take care of myself."

"Okay then." Was he the only awkward one here or was she simply aloof?

Dobson turned away and made her way outside.

Ha, that was annoying. She was definitely annoying. He didn't need that kind of person in his life now or ever, right?

CHAPTER 3

asper walked into his beach house and let out a long
breath. Just coming off a twenty-four-hour shift of two
twelve-hour days, his mind buzzed with what to do with
his days off.

His keys clattered as he dropped them onto the small metal tray
where he kept them, along with pennies and old cough drops. It was a
balmy June day and he wasn't about to spend it in bed catching up on
his sleep. Not when his sailboat and jet ski and other outdoor toys
called to him.

A growl in his stomach reminded him he'd not eaten lunch. He
checked his watch, and discovered his stomach had reason. Noon was
long gone and he hadn't eaten much for breakfast.

The refrigerator was pretty bare, except for yogurt and bottles of
fitness drinks. He grabbed a bottle and screwed off the lid. "All the
nutrition of a full, well-rounded healthy lunch in less than a minute."

He tossed the empty bottle in the garbage and stripped off his
clothes. Pulling on a pair of shorts and a T-shirt, a thought ran across
his brain. With his shift over, he had time to bother his brother Rhys.

He picked up his keys and went to his truck. Ten minutes later, he
was on the road and singing along with the song from the truck radio.

He headed to downtown Dunes Bay, where Rhys's tech business was located. He got out of the vehicle and stretched. The long shift was beginning to weary his bones and make him yawn.

He shoved open the door, setting off the little bell hanging on the door of Steele Tech Solutions. It would alert his brother when someone walked in, but not who. That's what outdated equipment did, or didn't do, for him. Rhys's business kept him too busy to care.

"Hey Jas, what are you doing here?" Rhys grabbed him in a brisk hug.

"Hey old man." Jasper teased, pretty impressed that he and his brothers excelled at teasing each other because they *practiced* regularly.

"So when did being thirty-five constitute being *old?*" Rhys frowned. "I'm wise in ways you can't understand, yet I'm agile and fit."

His oldest brother fast-footed in front him, punching at the air. "Oh, I forgot, oh master of nothing," Jasper said and brushed past Rhys on his way to the tiny kitchen. "I'm starved. Do you have anything good to eat?" He pulled open the fridge and shook his head. "Pitiful. I guess this apple will do."

"What do you expect? Are you here just for food or what's up?" Rhys went back to his office and dropped in to his seat in front of a computer screen.

"I don't know." Jasper parked beside him, leaning against the desk. "It's my day off. I want us to do something and I know Gray is busy putting together the newspaper."

Rhys sighed and leaned back in his chair. "I have a project I need to get done. Don't you have any project to do around your so-called home?"

"So called? You mean my beautiful cottage on the beach. Don't hate on the cottage," Jasper said.

Rhys chuckled. "Just kidding. You know I love chilling at your place. I guess I could take off the rest of the day."

Jasper stood up straight. "Let's go."

"Go where? What do you want to do?" Rhys enunciated each word slowly.

"I don't feel like swimming." He shivered. "The lake is too cold for me right now."

"How about we work on that window thing you asked me to help you with?"

"Work? You want to work?"

Jasper strode down the hallway out. "Again with attitude. You must not think much of me."

"Oh, I'm sorry." Rhys draped an arm over Jasper's shoulder. "I love you, man."

"Kidding! I know you're teasing. You know I'm willing do just about anything that involves working at your lighthouse." But he wasn't kidding about how his family's innocent barbs made him feel dismissed. Oh that's just Jasper, the screw-up. No one had ever said that. But his brothers were brilliant. He wasn't. He'd proven to them he was a screw up years ago. He allowed a good friend to drive under the influence, which led to a car wreck. The driver of the other vehicle was injured. Taking care of his friend, he took the blame because he hadn't been drinking and he had no priors. His family understood, he was, after all, the family's beautiful boy and that was all. He took the blame and got community service for the summer.

Jasper drove behind Rhys to his house on the lake. A warm breeze blew in his face when he got out of his truck. He breathed in the scents of water, sand, and freedom. That's what the lake was for him. It helped him survive the stress of seeing so much pain at work every day.

"C'mon." Rhys motioned him inside. "I'll get the supplies and meet you up top."

One foot after another, Jasper climbed up the winding stairs to the walkway around the lantern room. Looking out at the edge of the peninsula, he watched rolling waves slapping against the beach. He focused on the sounds of the waves and let it erase the tension in his shoulders. His house sat just off the beach among trees and offered its own kind of peace. But with the lighthouse, he never got tired of Rhys's place, and was grateful for access over the three years his brother had lived here. Memories rose of the many times Rhys, Gray, and he had engaged in conversations up top. Conversations that led to greater understanding of what they wanted their relationship to be like. They'd been best friends when they were just little boys driving their mom crazy. Luckily, they'd only gotten closer as adults, and still drove their parents nuts.

"Hey, a little help," Rhys called.

"Coming." Jasper took the stairs down to meet Rhys half-way, carrying a container of bolts and the replacement pieces of the steel railing as well as a box of tools. "Hand me something."

"Here, take the tools."

Back up at the top, Jasper picked up the reciprocating saw. "So you actually know what you're doing, right? I mean, you bring tourists up here. Aren't there specifications for this kind of thing?"

"Yes, I contacted a couple buddies from my days in the Coast Guard and got them." Rhys glared at him. "I do know what I'm doing."

After about a half hour taking out the rusted portion of the railing and bolting together the pieces of the new railing, Jasper wiped sweat off his brow. "It's hot out here."

"Yeah, I know. It's June. We're almost done." Rhys stretched his back. "I'm not promising anything, but maybe we could go fishing when we're done."

"Yeah, and call Gray. Maybe he could get away from the town newspaper at this afternoon to go with?"

"In fact, we need his boat."

Jasper laughed. "There is that." He knew Gray's boat was larger than Rhys's and his own.

He grabbed the last piece of steel and bolted it on while Rhys watched.

"It looks good. Sturdy. Now all we have to do is paint it."

Jasper turned to him and stared. "But you don't mean today. It's three o'clock. It's getting into our fishing time."

"No, painting can wait and I can do it alone. Thanks for your help. I'll give Gray a call." Rhys pulled his cell from his pocket. "It's ringing."

"Put him on speaker," Jasper said.

"Hey, Gray. Jas and I here at my house are ready to go fishing. Wanna come?"

"What you mean to say is, you want my boat."

Jasper chuckled. "Yes, exactly. And we want you. Can you go?"

"Sure. I could use a break. But remember, we're having dinner with Mom and Dad tonight."

Rhys exchanged a glance with Jasper. "Oh yeah. I forgot. Rachel keeps track of those kinds of things and just points me in the right direction."

"Of course, girlfriends and wives do that. Cherish does the same for me. Fishing at four o'clock? Meet me at my dock."

"Wait, I need to tell you something." Jasper's heart rate rose.

"Me?" Gray asked. "What is it?"

"I had a call at work earlier for a man who'd been shot. It was Devin Raye. I thought you and Cherish would like to know."

"Wow, that's, umm, startling. How is he?"

"He was in surgery this morning. Chances he'll survive are small, but it's possible. I don't know how Cherish will feel about it." Jasper cleared his throat. "Do you want me to tell her?"

"No, I'll do it. I'm not sure how she'll react. Thanks for the head's up." Gray was silent.

"Do you still want to go fishing?" Jasper asked.

"Yeah. So, meet at my dock at four?"

"Yup. See you soon." Rhys shoved his phone back in his pocket and Jasper started picking up. "We better hurry. It's almost four right now."

"We're having dinner en masse tonight?" Jasper scratched his head.

"Did you forget, too?"

Jasper winced. "Oh, man. I did forget. But I will have to skip it this time. I have a wedding to attend."

"You better call Mom." Gray chuckled with Rhys.

"I know," Jasper said. "I'll be sure to beg forgiveness for disappointing her."

Jasper grabbed his phone and called his mother. It was best to address it right away before he forgot.

"Hello," she answered.

"Hi Mom, I just need to say one quick thing." It was his way of attempting to forego a long conversation about her needs. "I can't make it tonight to dinner."

"Oh no. Why not?"

"I forgot I have a wedding reception to attend. The bride is a friend."

"Well, I'll miss you. But we wouldn't have planned the meal for tonight if I'd known you weren't going to make it."

Here it goes. The guilt trip that accompanied disappointment in him. "I understand. I just forgot. I hope you understand that I love you and promise not to miss the next family meal. You know I love your cooking?" he said, trying to cheer her up.

"Thank you for that. We'll all miss you. Have a good time at the wedding."

"I will. But I'll be missing the family. Bye."

It was a small thing. But the many times he'd failed her in her eyes stacked up. Nothing was easy with his mother. Every time he let her down he felt rejected, which he knew was his problem, not hers. Guilt shaded his heart. She was a wonderful mother; he had no right to feel blame her for his feelings of being invisible and especially invisible to her.

But he did.

* * *

THE PARTICULAR AROMA of the Dunes Bay Police Station hit Dobson as she walked in and went to her office. She loved the scent. Just as she loved her work.

She dropped her purse in a desk drawer and slapped her notebook onto the desk. If only her work loved her. From one misstep to another, she had stumbled her way through her first week at her new job. Today she continued, only what was different was that at the core of her stumbling stood Jasper, one of the most annoying, no, unnerving men she'd ever encountered.

Her notebooks stared her down. The only solution to her misery was to focus on the case and bring down Theodore Esposito's entire organization. No matter how many times she'd made that statement to herself, it remained true that 'Teddy' and his mob family were still out there doing all the criminal things they could, even from within the confines of prison. Teddy still had say so over whatever crimes were being committed and how. She'd seen phone call logs and heard from undercovers that he was very in touch.

"Sorry to disturb you, Dobson, but we need to talk."

"Of course. Come in, Chief." She swallowed hard. Here's when she would have to explain all her mistakes.

The tall, muscled man carrying a cup of coffee dropped into a chair on the other side of her desk. "I've been talking with others who are on the task force with you and according to them, you're doing a bang up job."

Her heart leapt and she did cartwheels in her head. "Thank you for sharing that. I'm very happy to hear that good news."

Chief Robert Nierling slouched in the chair but still dwarfed it. Easily more than six feet tall, he had to tilt his head down to look her in the eyes.

"How are you feeling about being here at DBPD?" he asked. "Are you getting to know your fellow officers? Are you getting acquainted with our beautiful town?"

"Everything is fine. I'm enjoying getting to know others in this department and in the town. I already have picked my favorite coffee shop, Coffee Easy." She stretched a smile across her face to give her statements more credibility. She had picked a place to buy coffee.

He took a sip of his coffee. "Our coffee isn't bad. You should try it."

"Oh, of course." Her mood wavered, and she sucked in her stomach and squared her shoulders. She couldn't even drink the right coffee?

"Well, like I said. We're happy to have you." His gaze drifted away. "I'm getting a lot of pressure from the press to get this Esposito case put to bed." He scrubbed his face. "How are you coming along?"

"I understand. As long as Teddy, some of his family, and cohorts are behind bars, the press should be glad their crimes are coming to an end." She pursed her lips. "The undercovers are keeping tabs on some of the members of the organization that are still free, and reporting back their activities to me. Very little of any weight has surfaced yet. But it will. I'm staying in touch with the Mosses. There's probably more to know about their connections."

Neirling nodded his head. "Sounds active. That's good." He leaned across her desk. "Hey, are you going to the reception tonight?"

"I don't know. I haven't decided yet." She caught herself chewing on her thumbnail and dropped her hands in her lap. Thoughts of the dress she'd bought *in case* she decided to go, circled in her brain.

"You should come." He uncrossed his legs and strode out the door.

Dobson blew out a breath. She shouldn't have authority issues, but her boss prompted more self-doubt. Her anxiety so easily took over, making her vulnerable. But she stomped on it and would never let it out in public if she could help it.

Her phone rang and she picked up. "Detective Ramirez," she announced.

"Hey, Dobson."

"Hi Zachary, what's up?"

"The task force needs to catch up. Can you do a meeting next Friday, at two o'clock?"

"Let's see. I'm checking my calendar." The only things on her calendar were work-related and there weren't very many. "Yes, I'm available."

"Great. We'll meet at the conference room at Delicious. Do you know where that is?"

"I'll find it. I'll see you then and there." The call from one of the FBI agents on the task force was strictly business and she liked it that way. She knew Chief Neirling's heart was in the right place when he encouraged her to settle in and get to know everybody. But secrets could be fatal, and getting too close to anyone would threaten hers.

CHAPTER 4

*D*obson followed the crowd of tuxedoed men and elegantly dressed women to the grand reception hall, reminding herself she belonged here just as much as her fellow Dunes Bay police officers. She knew Michael Shepard, the groom. Head detective, he'd introduced himself on her first day at the department. He stood tall at the bride and groom's table brandishing a huge smile and hugging his new wife.

Lyrics to the song *Walking on Sunshine* circled in her brain, scaring away fears of new people and new situations. She sort of believed in the chin-up philosophy, but got more encouragement from the *favorite things* focus. Sunshine, flowers, and really good coffee, to name a few.

Classical music poured into the hallway. She turned a corner into the reception room and caught her breath. Her eyes swept the room for familiar faces, but all she saw was strangers.

"Hey, newbie!"

Another DB officer waved at her. A small smile popped out, and Dobson waved back.

"Hi Hector." Dobson stepped closer to his table and eyed the name-cards sitting at each place at the full table.

"You're looking fine, detective." He chuckled.

"Well, look at you in your tux," she teased back. She knew he was right; she looked girlie and sexy, comforted in the blush pink, sleeveless short dress that hugged her body.

"This is my wife, Imani," Hector nodded his head toward the woman beside him. "Honey, this is the newest detective on the force, Dobson Ramirez."

"Nice to meet you, Imani."

The woman smiled up at Dobson. "It's nice to meet you. I hope the guys on the squad aren't giving you a bad time, you being new and all."

"No, not anything I can't handle," Dobson said, admiring the other woman's sparkly green gown and clear confidence. "I better find my seat."

"Save a dance for me," Hector called, and Dobson turned just in time to catch Imani slug him in the shoulder. The friskiness brought a smile to her lips.

She felt eyes turn to her as she strolled around scanning the tables for her name. Her heart hitched a bit, the frequent instinct to hide rising.

"Can I help you?"

Dobson raised her eyes to find a tall young man with sun streaked summer blonde hair and bright blue eyes that smiled at her. It was Jasper. "I'm okay. Just trying to find my seat."

"I'll help you. I haven't found mine yet either." He slanted his head. "Could we start over? Things started off a little rough with us."

His grin was welcoming and she couldn't ignore it. She smiled "My name is Dobson Ramirez. What's your name? I can help you too?"

"Jasper Steele. Nice to meet you, Dobson." His eyes engaged hers and stayed there.

His focus on her melted her into a pool on the floor. She wanted to trust him, but that was impossible. Even people she knew well didn't get her trust. Not after what had happened.

A quick toss of her long hair and the reminders she hated were gone. She could appreciate second chances. "We probably should find our seats quickly," she said, glancing around at the tables filling. She stepped away from Jasper toward another table and he followed on her heels.

She could sense him close by but when she rounded a table looking for her name and his, she noticed Jasper surveying another table. The music from a small strings and winds orchestra filled the air with beautiful notes that penetrated her reserve. Dobson pulled in a deep breath and relaxed her shoulders. This. This moment of peace was the reason she was in Dunes Bay, starting over.

"Well, look at this." Jasper motioned her in his direction. "I found your name."

"Thanks," she said, stepping over to the table where he stood beaming.

He held up the name card. "Read it."

She took the card from him. "Yup. My name." Her eyes surveyed the other guests already seated at the table and nodded her head. "Do you want me to keep looking for yours?"

"No, I happen to be sitting next to you," Jasper said, and picked up the card to show her. "How about that."

Dobson pursed her lips, suspicious. "Did you put that there?" Part of her wished he had and another part, the part she kept quiet inside, cringed. A reflex action she'd had since the *incident* that changed everything at her last job.

He pulled out her chair and motioned for her to sit. She hesitated a couple seconds, then her heart shifted. It might be fun to flirt a little. Hadn't she wished for a fun time to dispel the rut she was living in behind her walls?

"Thank you. Are you always this chivalrous?"

He tossed off her question with a lift of one shoulder. "You know," he said, and took the seat on her right. "I know only the cops here and I wasn't sure I wanted to come to the reception." He slanted his head and did that captivating thing with his eyes again, drawing her in. "Now I'm glad I'm here and sitting beside a new friend. Do you mind if I call you that?"

Her breath caught in her throat. Something in her wanted to shout, We're not friends! But her instincts told her he was simply being gracious. She liked that in people. "No. That's a nice thought." She took a sip of the champagne sitting at each place around the table.

"I'm optimistic. It's in my nature." He lifted a hand to wave at the bride.

"So you're a friend of the bride," she guessed. Another sip, and another was having a nice, warming effect on her.

"I am. What about you, bride or groom?" He lifted the champagne flute to his lips, his eyes gazing into hers over the rim of his glass.

"I work with the groom," Dobson said.

"I've met him because of my friendship with his new wife."

Dobson bit her lower lip. The conversation was casual, benign, but caution tightened her breath. "I've only been with the Dunes Bay Police Department for a short while." She started chewing on her lower lip. She couldn't help it. She'd vowed to behave better at her new job than the last, keep her distance, and here she was spilling her guts. Or so it felt.

Jasper's attention dropped to her lips and she stopped chewing immediately.

"I don't mean to fire questions at you," he said, leaning back in his chair.

Her heart squeezed. Her fears didn't have anything to do with him, not yet any way. So she smiled wide and went on. "I know that. We're just getting to know one another better. We might as well since we're both kind of on our own here."

The music got a little louder and faster and Dobson got chills watching the bride and her father take the dance floor. "Aww...so sweet," she said.

"They're pretty good. Personally, I could use a drink. Do you want me to get you something from the bar? It's free." He stood and waited for her answer.

"Yes I would. Surprise me."

"Oh, a woman who likes adventure," Jasper teased. "I'll be right back." He tossed her a grin and wove through the tables, his stance tall and his shoulders broad. Was she really ogling this blonde guy with the quick smile and easy going attitude, the same one who belittled her at the crime scene?

Applause pulled her attention back to the dance floor just in time to see the bride and her father bow to a round of cheers. The music changed to a romantic piece and the father gave the new husband his daughter's hand. Michael swept her in his arms and they danced slowly, with eyes only for each other.

The song sent melancholy trailing through her body. It was beautiful but it touched her in empty places, places that longed for that kind of interaction with her father but knew that would never happen. It was one of the *if only* musings she usually stuffed deep. Things like a father-daughter dance, a father's admiration and support —those hadn't been hers for a very long time. She accepted that long ago. But. Sometimes the loss of him got close to the surface where it tugged at her heart.

"Mesmerized?" Jasper interrupted her thoughts.

She shook her head for a second to bring her thoughts back to the present and accepted the tall glass he handed her. "It's a pretty pink," she said, then took a sip. "Mmm…delicious."

"It's a berry rosé mojito."

"That would explain the strawberries and rosé. Thank you." She tasted it and licked her lips. "It's good."

Just then servers came to their table and set plates of food in front of them. "I see you got the salmon," he said.

"And you got the steak. Are you a meat and potatoes man?" The idle chatter was getting on her nerves, but it was all she had at the moment.

"I'm what you would call a "food man.' I like food in general. Give me a juicy cheeseburger, some fresh sushi, or a bowl of garden vegetables sautéed in olive oil and I'll be happy."

"I'm a meat and potatoes guy," chimed in a man who pulled out a chair and sat down at the table.

"I can attest to that," said the woman beside him. "I'm Lizzy and this is my husband Sam."

"It's nice to meet you. I'm Jasper."

Their presence jolted her out of her absorption with Jasper. "I'm Dobson." She pointed to Jasper. "We're not together."

"Oh, but you make such a nice couple," Lizzy cooed. "Surely you have some things in common."

A younger man and woman filled the last remaining seats. "I'm Mia and this is my boyfriend David." The twenties-something smiled at her boyfriend and he nodded.

"Nice to meet you all," he said, rising again. "Excuse us, these are our seats, but we're going to dance."

"Great. The orchestra is wonderful." Jasper watched them walk away, then turned back to the table. "We just met." Jasper nodded his head at her.

"Right. So we might have things in common but we wouldn't know." Dobson stumbled over the words that tumbled out of her mouth. It could have been the alcohol loosening her guards and making her vulnerable.

"Well, hell, this might just be the opportunity of a lifetime for you to get to know each other." Sam winked at them and chuckled. "Both of you from around here?"

This is what her life was; chit chat about steak and fish, whether she and Jasper had thing in common, and pink mojitos? She tuned inward. A remnant from childhood still affected her. It was an expectation of being dismissed that never failed to spiral her down. She bit her lip, trying to quiet the old fears of being on the outside. Her skin prickled at the idea of walking around trying to connect with the other officers at the reception. She swallowed hard. But that's why you're here.

"Excuse me." A young man interrupted the conversation. "Dobson, remember me?"

"Of course. You're Officer Jordan," she said.

"I'm glad you made it to this gig. The guys and I have been talking over there." He nodded his head to the back of the room. "You're welcome to join us, but I see ole' Jasper has taken over your time." He punched Jasper in his arm.

"He has been very…fun." Dobson shot him a look. "I'd love to sit with you all." She waved at the group of her fellow detectives. "I'll catch up with you soon."

"Sure. You shouldn't leave this one alone. He's quite the player." Jordan winked at Jasper.

"You don't say." Dobson ran her eyes up and down his body.

"Jordan you're full of shit." Jasper shook his head. "You don't know what you're talking about."

Jordan hit him playfully in the arm again. "Just kidding, man." He pointed at Jasper. "He's a fine EMT and a good guy."

Dobson's eyes were on Jasper's. Men could be so hard on each other. "Well, we just met, so no worries."

In Jordan's wake, her thoughts bounced from ignoring the title—that he was a player—or shooting it down. Did it matter?

"I hope I can be redeemed by own recognizance.

Jasper's attempt at making a joke fell flat on the floor in front of her, but she shot him a smile anyway.

His eyes fluttered briefly and he fidgeted with his napkin. "My brothers and I fish. Do you ever go out on the lake to catch the big one?"

Dobson's gaze collided with Jasper's and she realized she had lost track of the conversation. "Me? Fish? On Lake Michigan? No." Her 'no' came out loud, more emphatic than she meant.

"So that's a no, then." Jasper's lips lifted slightly at the corners.

We've gone from introductions to mocking me again? "I never have but I expect as long as I'm in living near the lake I'll fish some-time." Blush warmed her face, but she stared straight ahead at Sam and Lizzy engrossed in conversation, then came back to land on Jasper. "If I get the occasion."

Jasper seemed determined to open her up. "So you're not a fishing enthusiast and you haven't been on the lake. What are you doing in Dunes Bay?"

"I needed a change of scenery," Dobson said, and gave a small smile. It was the truth. She sucked in a deep breath. Weariness shud-dered through. She'd been restraining her spontaneity for so long that crying, or screaming, or grabbing the moment to do something crazy threatened to burst out of her. She gritted her teeth, vowing never to let it all out again. She'd done that and it didn't work out well.

"You've found very nice scenery here," Lizzie said. "Lake Michigan is awesome. It can be calm and beautiful or slowly rolling and inviting or furious and stormy. And of course the dunes are graceful and timeless."

Lizzie's words struck Dobson as absurd given her state of mind as she struggled to pay attention. "I haven't introduced myself to the dunes, but I'm eager to." She shivered, knowing very well that the water temps in the lake stayed cold almost all year though she could get into a swim.

"Enough talk about the scenery," Sam declared. "Lizzie what say you and me get drinks." He pulled out her chair and they walked hand and hand toward the bar.

Jasper sighed heavily. "I think Sam was ready for a breather." He turned to her directly.

"You're probably right. I'm not the world's best conversationalist." She moved her glass to line up with the utensils.

"Oh, I think you're very people-friendly." He leaned his chin on his hand and gave her a look.

"You seem to hit it off with him. I'm not really a people person. I like people, but, well…" She let the sentence drop. "I'm tired of talking about myself."

"So let's dance," he said. "Would you like to dance with me?"

How could she ignore his disarming demeanor and turn down his offer? "I would like that."

CHAPTER 5

Jasper took her hand in his, noting the softness of her skin, and led her to the dance floor. She stood a step away and moved her body to the beat of the music. A sense of joy filled him and he couldn't suppress another smile. He thought he'd never smiled so much, but he couldn't stop. He'd written her off earlier. But now she was enchanting. She did something inexplicable to him that he couldn't ignore.

The music stopped mid-dance moves and began a slow song. Personally, he was all for it. She piqued his curiosity for what it would be like to hold her in his arms. She eyed him and he pulled her close as they stepped into a gentle sway to the dreamy mix of the strings and piano.

Dobson tilted her head back and captured his gaze. "This is nice." She shifted a little closer in his arms, and a delicious whiff of her skin filled his head. It wasn't too flowery or overwhelming and he imagined her soaping up in the shower.

Whoa, whoa, man. You just met this woman. Tone it down.

Jasper blew out a long breath. "I'm enjoying it." He smiled. Crap, there I go again. He virtually shook his head. "Do you mind if I say your eyes are beautiful?"

"Of course not." She laughed. "They're just ordinary brown eyes. And may I say I think your smile is very nice."

"You're going to make me blush, but thank you." What is happening? Are we flirting? He was pretty sure they were, and he liked it. Suddenly an image popped up of Dobson lying in bed with her hair haloed around her head, looking all funky and relaxed, and his heart stuttered.

"The music is amazing," Dobson said. "I used to play the flute."

Her words interrupted his chain of thought. He swallowed hard. "Really?" She seemed not to notice his mind had been somewhere else entirely.

"In my family it was never, *do* you want to play an instrument? It was *which* instrument do you want to play?"

"My family wasn't musical, but I can whistle," he chuckled. "I'm dancing with a flutist. Never done that before. But this music is romantic." He pulled her a little closer.

"Yes, romantic." She slowly lowered her eyelids and nuzzled into his neck.

Her silky soft hair brushed his cheek and his private vision of her expanded. His mouth went dry and his senses reveled in her scent, her warmth, the feel of her curves pressed against his body.

Taking a leap is easier when an attractive woman has overwhelmed your inhibitions, he decided, and whispered in her ear. "I want to make love to you. Right now."

Her eyes flew open but she didn't pull away or stop dancing. She turned her gaze on him. "Now?"

"Yes," he said lowly, "I know we just met, so of course this is wild and crazy."

"Completely mad," Dobson said, while staring wide-eyed at him with a small grin lifting her lips.

Jasper's heart stuttered. He knew that look on a woman's face, but it had been a while since he'd been moved by it. Was she interested in casual, mad, passionate sex? With him? "I know a place we can let down our," he cleared his throat, "hair."

Dobson pulled a hairpin out of her hair. It draped into long, soft waves, and he couldn't breathe.

He dropped his arms to his sides, took hold of one of her hands, and headed out of the reception room with her by his side.

"We must be insane," she muttered.

"Officially." He nodded and wrapped an arm over her shoulders.

She walked with him down a hall and around a corner. His heart pounded in his chest. Anticipation bloomed. *God, Jasper, you'd think this was your first time.* If he were truthful with himself he'd have to face the facts: he'd been intimate with a number of women, but it was always the same. If he'd been a toad with yellow teeth and warts all over his face, would they have shown him a minute of their time? He accepted that he had looks, but beyond that, he might as well have been invisible. He'd never truly connected with anyone.

"You okay with this?" Dobson asked. "You seem lost in something."

"I'm more than okay," he quickly answered. "My thoughts are on you." He lifted his eyebrows a couple times and Dobson laughed.

"Where is this place you mentioned?" Her eyes darted from one doorway with Employees Only on it to another with a sign that read Janitor Office.

Urgency shivered through him. The feelings they both seemed to sense could slip away, leaving them staring at each other wondering how they got there instead of enjoying an afterglow.

Jasper marched toward another door with a sign that read Consultation and tried the knob. It turned in his grasp and the door opened.

"Oh." Dobson voice lilted. She crept up behind him and peeked past his shoulder. "This could work."

"I had a call in this venue one time and noticed this room because people were in here talking." They tip-toed inside the room and stopped. Jasper took in the chairs, couch, and desk, while Dobson pulled the door closed, locked it, and leaned against it.

Silence flowed between them and time stalled as Jasper's nerves jumped like a live wire.

"We're doing—" she began.

In two long quick steps he closed the gap between them and took hold of her shoulders, stopping her mid-sentence with a decisive kiss. Her arms swept around him and his lips drove a long, sensual kiss to her lips.

"Yes, we're doing this," he said when the kiss ended.

She let out a long breath and he cupped her face, his breaths coming harder, deeper. "You're more than beautiful, you're interesting."

Before she could respond he brushed her lips with his, and savored the soft feel of them.

Dobson kicked off her shoes and he followed, then she slipped the sleeves of her gown off each shoulder. He kissed each one as she leaned back her head so he could gently kiss her neck. The sweet smell of carnations wafted faintly around her.

He shivered while she quickly unbuttoned his shirt and pressed her lips to his chest, then trailed them down to his waistline. He took hold of her and shoved her against a wall, his desire surging. All the frustrations of the last few days sparked into passion.

"Jasper, you smell so good," she murmured, and tucked her fingers just inside his waist band, then rubbed her thumb over his belly.

Her eyelids drifted closed and he lifted her dress over her head, exposing lacy, pink underwear.

"Oh my God, woman," he said, his voice husky.

She opened her eyes wide. "Fast and furious?" she asked softly.

He kissed her hard, with all the passion steaming inside driving him. The straps of her bra slipped off her shoulders, and he cupped her breasts, then swiftly unhooked it.

He unbuckled his pants and tossed them aside impatient to feel her curves next to his skin. "So fast and furious," he agreed, and took one breast in his mouth, then the other.

He pushed his body against her and every nerve inside him cried for release.

CHAPTER 6

*D*obson reveled in the excitement of skin against skin. Jasper's hard abs pressed against her belly, coaxing her to let loose her inhibitions and all thoughts of what was right, what was wrong.

A fervent kiss sent her head spinning, and the touch of his hands on her breasts heightened her reverie. Everything in her surrendered to the here and now.

He traced her curves and she kicked off her underwear.

"You're killing me here Dobson," he groaned.

Her fingers grasped his hardness, exhilaration spiraling through her. Her heightened senses were keenly aware that someone could knock on the door and they'd have to scramble. That awareness exhilarated her pulse.

"I'm not stopping you," she said.

At that, he thrust inside her, and her mind narrowed to a tiny point of light where only the two of them existed. Their rhythmic movements matching, seconds flew by and then they came together. Everything trembled, and holding onto each other they slipped to the floor. Dobson lay on the floor entangled with Jasper cuddling, bliss humming through her.

Minutes passed in silence as she caught her breath. Then Jasper spoke, but his words were muffled with his face in the crook of her neck and her hair splayed across it.

He lifted his head. "I'm speechless." His eyes beamed and he shifted his weight off her, propping his head on his hand.

She shook her head slowly. "Never have I ever…" she said, her words falling off.

Jasper chuckled and stroked her cheek. "Made love in the midst of a wedding reception?" he finished for her.

She ran her finger down the bridge of his nose. "That's not what I meant."

His smile dropped and his gaze sombered. "I know. Me either. This was phenomenal." He slanted his head and kissed her softly.

Breathless, Dobson had to admit this spontaneous sex with Jasper was supremely delicious. Key word, spontaneity. It was freeing and spacious, feelings she'd never experienced before. She wanted to savor the moment and just lie in Jasper's arms. Not think about work, or her coworkers, or…her father, her mother, or her affair. "I suppose we should get our clothes on and get back to the reception before someone comes looking for us," she said.

"Oh, don't say that," he groaned, but pushed up and offered her a hand, pulling her to her feet. "I'll never forget this time."

"You sound like you're leaving for Australia or something." Dobson draped her arms around his neck and her senses re-fired.

But she knew the moment was done, and dropped her arms to her side.

"I'm not going anywhere. Dunes Bay is my home town. I'm born and raised here in Dunes Bay. My work is here. My family is here." He pulled on his pants and wrestled into his shirt and suit coat.

"Got it. You're never leaving Dunes Bay." She grabbed her dress and shimmied into it. The panic in Jasper's voice gave her a clear message. He wanted a brief encounter. That's all. The fun, little fling was turning weird. She stepped into her strappy shoes and picked up her purse.

"Stop." He touched her shoulder. "I was simply voicing my feelings. I didn't mean to sound like I was blowing you off. I'm sorry."

"No apologies necessary. We agreed to have a little fun and now the thing is done." She flashed him the biggest smile she could.

"Wait." Jasper stood in her path. "Yes this was amazing and fun, but I would really like to get to know you."

He looked directly at her and she saw nothing but warmth and sincerity. Her heart pounded hard in her chest. Could she trust this stranger not to turn her life into a nightmare? Like before. "What would that look like?"

"We could go back to the reception and just talk, you know, learn more about each other. Become friends."

She darted her eyes from one corner of the room to another and clamped down on the voices in her head warning her to protect herself.

She cleared her throat and tuned out all the confusion and panic. "I could do that." She sighed. "I mean, what would be the harm in that?"

Jasper chuckled. "Well, that's not an enthusiastic response but I understand." He pulled on his suit coat without dropping his gaze.

"Thank you for that." Confusion was speaking for her, but she couldn't help it. "You know, I've never done this before with anyone. Flings are not my thing."

He took her hand and raised it to his lips to place a kiss there. "Me either. In fact, I haven't been intimate with a woman for some time."

He dropped his gaze and stared at the floor, and she deduced that he wasn't quite recovered from something hurtful. Her heart softened as he became more someone real, not just the *fling* she had at a wedding.

He lifted his eyes and shrugged. "Well, Dobson Marie Perez Ramirez, thank for this exquisite evening. Shall we get out of this room before we're discovered?"

Panic quieted and Dobson gathered her things as well as her optimism, and walked out the door allowing herself to enjoy anticipation of possibilities.

·   ·   ·

THEY RESUMED the evening at the same table. Jasper pulled out the chair for Dobson and slipped into the chair beside her. Electricity sparked just under his skin. He'd been truthful. He'd never had a fling and over the last year he'd stayed away from dating. Burned by his former girlfriend's infidelity, he'd sworn off relationships. Sometimes something can be so painful one could never jump back in. That's how it had been with her, his former girlfriend.

"Champagne?" A server with a tray of full flutes leaned toward them.

"Perfect timing." Jasper grabbed two, one for him and one for Dobson, and thanked the server. He took a sip and met her eyes over the top of the glass. They were so direct he almost choked on the tingly liquid.

"Oh, are you all right?" she asked and handed him a napkin. "Did the bubbles get to you?"

Something got to me but not the champagne. "Something like that. How about a toast?"

"To us," she said, and clinked his glass.

"To us, and our possible friendship."

It got quiet between them and he wracked his brain for chit chat, at least. Their uneaten plates of food still sat in front them, prompting an idea. "Hey, do you want to get out of here? Our food is cold. How about we go to a place I know and get a sandwich or something?"

Dobson nodded. "I'm in."

"I'll drive and you can follow, okay?"

Jasper strode through the door at the diner and held it open for Dobson. He directed her to a booth in the back by a window. "So, should we talk about it?"

A waitress set glasses of water on the table. "Hi Jasper. Who's your friend?" She eyed Dobson.

"Tricia, this is Dobson, Dobson, Tricia."

Tricia smiled and they exchanged pleasantries. She nodded in the direction of the wall over the grill. "That's our menu."

"We'll need a minute, right?" Jasper asked.

"Yes, thank you."

He grabbed his glass and guzzled the water. He peered at her. She was exquisite and their time together had been hot. Wow! He pulled at his collar. He decided to bypass his initial question to her. "So, you're new in town. How long have you been here? Where is home for you?" He leaned closer across the table and got a whiff of her delicate flowery fragrance. She made his thoughts spin.

She let out a sigh. "It's been a long Friday."

He gave her a chance to collect her thoughts in silence.

"I'm from Chicago. I moved to Dunes Bay three weeks ago."

"Okay." He let that process. She was a big city girl. "I already told you I'm a native of Dunes Bay. Population 80,000, give or take."

"Yes, I know, fully know. And your family is here too. My family consists of my mother and me. We lived in Chicago, in Lincoln Park, to be specific. I worked on the Chicago Police Department."

"I know officers from the CPD. Small world, huh?" Jasper said. His gaze strayed from her face and took in the landscape outside the window. Reminiscing brought up his friend from high school, Riley Phelps. His heart heavied.

"Small world. In fact, I came to Dunes Bay to get away from Chicago."

Was it just him or did she flinch? Curiosity spun through him, but he was too busy extracting his foot from his mouth to inquire. "Chicago's loss? What do you do on the DBPD?"

"I came here specifically because I have experience working with organized crime." Dobson took a drink of water. "I have taken on a case here in that area."

Now it was his turn to flinch. Was Dobson working on the Moss case, he wondered. Geez, would that state of affairs never go away? "What, we have organized crime in Dunes Bay? Say it ain't so." He feigned shock, all the while knowing Gray's wife and his sister-in-law and her sister had been on pins and needles since their parents had become state's witnesses testifying about their involvement with the Esposito crime organization.

"Unfortunately, yes. These people are like cockroaches. They're everywhere." She sipped her drink and refocused on him. "And you're an EMT."

"I am. My work is probably as thrilling as yours is." His gut knotted, thinking about his work.

"That's amazing. You must feel so proud of what you do. I feel that too, but in a different way I'm sure."

"Yes, it is my privilege to help people and save lives, but the work can get to me. I don't like seeing people hurt and I don't like death." Dread at the thought of his next shift thudded in the pit of his stomach. But he knew blood and loss of life were what he had signed up for when he became an emergency medical tech.

"You're a hero. I admire your work." Dobson touched his hand.

"No," he protested. "I'm just an average guy doing his job. A job that is sometimes, no frequently, heartbreaking. "I am impressed with your courage. Boy, fighting against the mob, that's a scary one."

"I get an adrenaline kick out of putting bad guys away. But it's frustrating that even in prison they manage to keep their fingers in places they don't belong."

Jasper ran his fingers through his hair. "I can see how your job is harder than mine. My patients are readily available. You have to go after your subjects."

"And, they probably aren't going to kill you," she added.

"That's not totally true. I've run into quite uncooperative patients. Plus they can be really messed up or dead."

"Oh, I never thought about that." She gave him a very small smile.

He hadn't meant to bring the conversation to a dark place, but that was his work life. Jasper squirmed inwardly. Silence stretched palpably between them. He took a sip of coffee and another bite of his turkey sandwich. He chewed slowly but didn't taste the sandwich much. Disrupted thoughts and emotions pinballed in his chest.

"How's your salad?" he asked her, to end the uncomfortable silence.

"Good. I'll have to put this place on my lists of restaurants I like." Dobson lowered her gaze and stared into her coffee.

The obvious swirled around them and he couldn't bare the weight of it. Maybe they'd moved way to fast, but at least they should address it.

"Let's talk about it." Jasper dropped his voice a notch. "I mean, don't you think we should?"

She shrugged. "I don't have any regrets. Do you—"

He jumped on her question. "No. I don't have any regrets either." He repressed an urge to take her hand in his to assure her she was safe. Following her lead would be the right thing, not invading her space without being asked.

"Jasper, our encounter was lovely. You were lovely. But I don't do flings."

"Today was your first fling?"

She blinked, blinked, blinked.

"It's all right. We're just talking." Jasper's heart pounded. He sensed she was close to flight. Why was he trying so hard to prevent her from it, convince her stay?

She skewered him with her gaze. "You're right. To be direct, I think I like you. But we jumped ahead. One minute we hated each other and the next we were having sex."

Jasper made a face. "Well, I wouldn't say I hated you."

"You surely can admit I irritated you."

He laughed and she chuckled with him. It was like fresh air after a storm. "I plead the fifth. The important thing is I like you too. I'm not necessarily looking for a long-term relationship. I have too many dangerous things to do before I settle down." He wadded up his paper napkin and tossed it on the table. "I can't imagine not seeing you again."

"Is that the sex talking?" Dobson shook her head. "How could it be anything but that at this point?"

Her eyes pleaded with him. It took him a minute to grasp that something really bad had happened to her. He would have to earn her trust. He had to be honest.

"No," he said softly. "No doubt I'm attracted to you. I'm not dead.

But it's more than that. I think we can have good times and see where things go. Can you do that?"

"It's not easy to get to know me but I would like that." A sparkling smile stretched across her face and his heart tripped in response. This was going to be interesting.

CHAPTER 7

As she brewed coffee, Dobson heard her mom stirring around in her bedroom down the hall from the kitchen. Her mother's sounds gave her a homey feel. She relaxed into her mom's presence, at least as relaxed as she was capable of getting.

Her eyes fluttered at a passing thought of Jasper, but she let it go quickly. She drew in a breath, lifted her chin, and put on a smile.

"Mom, coffee is about ready," she called from the kitchen. "Let's sit for a few minutes before I have to go to work." Waiting, she ran her eyes over the kitchen décor. The plain white walls didn't inspire her, and the whole room needed an update. She shrugged. There would be time for that…sometime. She made a mental note to paint this month. Time was passing in turbocharge these days.

Her mom walked into the kitchen and went straight to the window. "It looks like a nice Saturday morning out there, sweetie. If the temperature isn't too hot I may sit on the balcony and make more progress on the scarf I'm crocheting for you."

"It's definitely not scarf weather now," Dobson said.

She set two cups of coffee on the tiny kitchen table and pulled out a chair for her mother.

"Thanks. You're so good to me," her mother said, sitting across from Dobson.

She reached out and took her mom's hand. It was bony, just like the rest of her body. She pushed the thought of her mother's lung cancer out of her mind. "I love you." Her words choked in her throat.

Her mother's eyes stared into Dobson's and they shared a silent knowing of what would come sooner than either of them wanted.

Cecilia Marie Perez Ramirez, her mother, was dying.

"Mija, let's not get sad. Don't worry about me."

"Mamá, you are never out of my thoughts." She couldn't suppress the sorrow that chewed on her gut all the time; walking through her days, quickening her pulse at the idea of her mom leaving her. A tear escaped and she quickly brushed it away.

"No estés triste."

"Don't die and I won't be sad."

"I can't make promises," her mom said.

"I know. Well, I better get going," Dobson said, and finished her coffee.

"It's Saturday. You're going to work today?"

She gathered her things and kissed her mom on the top of her head. "Have to. You have a good day, Mamá."

She pulled her car into the street and tried to shed the melancholy.

Traffic in Dunes Bay never presented problems. Traffic *jams* rarely occurred, so this day as with every day, she drove the ten minutes to her office without delays. Work was close enough she could walk, but she didn't trust the weather.

Her heart flitted on her way through the front door. Several officers were gathered chattering at the front desk area. Her heels tapping on the tiled floor grabbed their attention.

"Morning, Dobson. You working a Saturday?" Hector lifted his head in hello and others murmured theirs and shot her smiles. Her nerves settled at the welcoming signs. It was so different from what had happened after the Big Deal and every cop in the district turned on her.

"Who needs a day off?" she joked.

"I do." Michael Shepard raised his hand and the others gave him a good laugh.

"How's married life going for the newlyweds, Michael?" she asked in passing.

"I have no complaints," he said, grinning ear to ear.

In her office, she didn't bother to sit down. Plans for the morning lay out in front of her and eagerness pushed her to get on the road. She clipped her badge to her belt and grabbed her notebook from a drawer and stuffed it in her purse. "Here I come, Teddy," she said out loud.

DOBSON USED the two-hour drive to the prison for practicing her interview with Teddy. The time flew by, and soon she walked up to the Danigan Street Correctional Facility visitor door and thanked her lucky stars she'd never committed a felony. From its tall fencing surrounding the prison to the guard tower standing tall and always watching, the place sucked up the air all around.

The first time she'd met Teddy was in Chicago and she hadn't actually met him. He was pointed out to her while in a restaurant with an FBI agent, discussing his criminal network. From across the room she could see his soulless, piercing dark eyes and knew he was dangerous. It was in that meeting that she'd learned the FBI wanted her working in Dunes Bay.

"Ms., are you here to visit a prisoner?" The guard's face was emotionless.

She showed him her badge. "Yes, Teddy Esposito. I'd also like to get a visitor's list and phone log for him, please."

"I'll have your list ready in just a minute. Sign in right here."

He pointed to the screen on the shelf and she entered her name, her thoughts drifting to the upcoming interaction with the mob boss. Her breaths were coming fast, so she deliberately slowed them down. She had to remain vigilant not to give away a tell while with Teddy. She tightened her lips into a straight line and forced her self-confidence to take control.

"Her you go, detective. Here's the list."

"Thank you."

Another guard walked to the visitor's space. "So you're seeing Teddy?"

"Yes, I have a few questions for him."

The guard chuckled as they walked to the visitor's room. "He's a crafty one. I suggest you be polite and respectful or he'll take you down."

Dobson didn't blink. "Thanks for the advice."

"He'll be here in just a few minutes. You can sit right there." He pointed to a cubicle with a telephone and a stool.

"Okay." She sat on the stool and ran her hands over her pants. She knew to expect nothing and be surprised at cooperation. He would have no incentive to give her information, so she had to find a way to convince him it was to his benefit to talk. She traced the lines around the bricks on the opposite wall and waited for the door to open. The air was cold, and she didn't hear voices in the room. It almost felt private here behind the Plexiglas.

The door opened and a guard escorted Teddy into the room and sat him down across from her on the other side of the Plexiglas. Chills rippled through her that were unrelated to the cold.

Their eyes met and he laughed. They each put a receiver to their ear to communicate.

"Detective Ramirez. Aren't you pretty." He pounded a quick beat on the desk top. "Nice of you to visit me."

He could try but he could not get under her skin. The last thing she'd do is react to his remarks.

"We've never met. How did you know it was me?"

"I read the newspaper."

"Ah, you've seen my picture. I must say, it's nice to see you…in this place." She stared at his dark eyes and opened her notebook. "Let's get started." If she knew anything about Teddy it was that his goal was always to win and get the upper hand. He'd already tried to exert the power of his presence.

"What country are you from?" she asked, looking steadily into his eyes.

Teddy frowned and moaned. "You know I'm a native of Nicaragua. Stop wasting my time."

She twirled her pen and smiled. "I'm just trying to get all the facts. I never assume."

"Well, you can assume this. I'm about ready to call the guard." His face settled into a seething, tight smile.

She tapped her pen on the desk and perused her questions, dragging out the minutes just to annoy him. "How long have you been the head of the Esposito's crime organization?"

He exploded and jumped to his feet. "I'm innocent of any and all wrong doing and so is my business."

Guards rushed him and grabbed his arms. They made to escort him out.

"It's okay," Dobson said. "No harm done. I'm not finished with my interview."

The guards slammed him into his seat. "We'll be watching you," one guard warned.

"You and I both know you just lied. Now, if you don't like that question, we'll move to another one. Are you an American citizen?"

Teddy sighed heavily. "Yes. So are all of my family."

Dobson bided her time, waiting for the right moment. She perused the lists the guard had given her for familiar names.

"I see you've had a number of visits and calls with Marco and your nephews, Franco and Robby Ricci. What did you discuss with them?"

Coolly, he eyed her. "Just visits. You know, family matters."

"Is your base of operation is in the U.S.?"

Teddy shifted in his seat, restless. "You know these things." He didn't raise his voice but his annoyance signaled Dobson that it was time.

"Just one more question, then we'll be done." She shot him a meaningless smile and waited two beats. "Why did you have Devin Raye shot?"

His eyes flicked and his face got red. "I did not ask anyone to kill

Devin. He's one of my best clients and a damn fine man." He got up to leave.

"Sit down. I'm not done."

"You said you only had one more question. Asked and answered," he growled.

"Are you involved with Adrian and Emma Moss in a professional way?" Her words were stern, but she didn't care. She'd gotten what she wanted, which was a reaction to her question about Devin. Bonus, he'd misspoken and used the word *kill*. But she wouldn't tell him Devin was alive. He would send his goons to make sure this time he wouldn't be able to talk.

"I'm done. I thought this meeting would interrupt the daily boredom, but I'm bored right now, Dobson, sweetie."

She slammed her hands down on the table. "Don't call me that. I'm not your sweetie. And I say when we're done."

Teddy eyed the guards through the window in the door, then turned back to face her. "I know what you're doing. You're trying to get me in trouble."

"You're already in deep shit. Now, tell me who your contact is on the outside. Who is doing your dirty work for you?"

He smirked. "Help me understand why you think I could run things from inside these walls."

"I have proof." She'd confirmed by the information she'd gotten from the guard that he was working through his family, but it would be something if he would amidst that to her. "I assure you, your reach into the community will get cut off soon. Nice talking with you." She picked up her briefcase and stood. "Now we're done." A quick motion to the guards and they began to take Teddy back to his cell.

He managed to rip out of their grasps and came straight toward her. She took steps backward.

Before they could get a hold on him he slammed his hands against the window and it rattled but remained in place.

"You bitch! You'll know when I'm done with you," he hollered while struggling with the guards. "You'll be dead."

* * *

It wasn't always easy getting to sleep any more. Images of individuals dead and dying haunted him and trying to put them out of his mind was getting harder. To help his brain dismiss the images from last night, Jasper spent the morning watching a mind-numbing movie on TV and now his legs ached from sitting so long. The weather app on his phone said the temperature was a balmy seventy-five degrees with a six mph breeze. Maybe he could borrow Koda, Gray's dog, and go for a good run. He decided to ask Cherish because he could also check with her that Gray had told her about Devin.

He punched in her name in favorites and waited.

"Hi Jasper." Gray's wife Cherish sounded cheery.

"Hi. Say, I'm calling for two reasons. Am I catching you at a busy time?"

"No, I'm just sitting here in my gorgeous new office going through trial notes on my day off. What's up?"

"I'd like to take Koda for a run this afternoon. Would that be okay?"

"Of course. Koda would love that. You know the code for the front door, right?"

"Yes. I'll probably be by your house early after lunch. Thanks."

"What's the second question?"

"It's not a question. Umm…I just didn't know how you'd feel—"

"About what?" she interrupted.

He ran his hand through his hair and gritted his teeth. "Did Gray tell you about Devin Raye?"

"He did," she said, her voice dipping. "I don't know how I feel either. I mean, I don't wish him harm, but he was living on the edge, working with the Esposito crime organization. I'm not surprised, I guess." Her voice trailed off.

"I know. That's how I feel too. He might not make it."

Silence hung between them. Jasper waited, giving her a chance to catch her breath.

"I-I don't know what to say. Where is he? Gray must have told me but I don't remember."

"Dunes Bay Hospital. He was in surgery late yesterday. There was a slim chance at that point that he would survive."

"You're so kind, Jas. I'll sort out my feelings, but I'm very glad you called. I thought I would see you at dinner last night at the folks' house. I missed you. You and your crazy humor keep things lively."

He laughed. "I'm sure you all had a lively time without me. But you're right. I am a funny guy."

"You're more than that, Jasper. Humor is only one of your attributes."

"Oh really? Well, go on. I'd like to hear them all," he joked.

"You nut. I need to get back to work. Have fun with Koda."

CHAPTER 8

Jasper picked up Koda and drove to the beach, anticipation of getting some good exercise and sunshine stirring in his stomach. Exhilaration was his go to state of being and he found it often in nature.

He opened the door for Koda and didn't have to coax much. "C'mon boy. Let's do a run." Koda immediately scrambled out of the car and hit the ground running.

"Whoa, wait for me, boy!" he called. Koda came running back and licked Jasper's leg. "Good boy."

Jasper strode to the beach where the water met the sand. Sunshine sparkled on the lake, drawing him in. He tilted back his head, closed his eyes and enjoyed the warmth of the sun on his face. He let out a breath and breathed in the fresh scent of the lake. The sounds of the water sizzling against the water's edge echoed through the tension in his body and he relaxed into it.

"Stretches first, Koda." He did a couple stretches, savoring the nature setting he was so fortunate to take advantage of.

"Let's go," he said to Koda, and the dog took off running beside him.

Getting out into nature was a family thing. He wasn't the only one who lived on the lake. Gray and Rhys were just as fond of the active lake life as he was. But they rarely ran together. Running was a private thing for them when they could deeply connect with the earth's rhythms. He never questioned where that mutual affinity came from, he just knew it was there.

He ran past the mountainous sand dunes, his breath coming hard. Koda's huffing breaths sounded beside him. "Isn't this great? You're holding a good pace, boy."

The sun beat on his bare back, heating his skin. He ran by the peninsula where Rhys's lighthouse stood tall and beautiful. Pushing harder, he kept his pace steady by challenging it. His feet thudded on the wet sand, running by Steele's Small Engine and Boat Repair near the marina where their boats bobbed serenely in the water. Euphoria filled him. Jasper let a burst of energy push his pace faster. "Keep up, Koda."

Breathing hard, he approached the public beach, where swimmers and sunbathers languished. It was a Saturday, so of course the beach was full. He wove around people standing on the edge of the water, chatting in small groups, and playing with children. One child splashed in the water vigorously as he ran past.

"Koda, be careful. Watch for the people." Koda ran father into the water, splashing and drinking, while Jasper ran in place. Jasper scooped a handful of water and splashed Koda with it. Koda assumed a play position. "Oh no, no, we're not playing. Let's move on." He slapped his thigh and took off running through little pools of captured water amidst the sand. Jasper could hear Koda's splashing behind him and smiled. He loved that dog.

"Akk!"

He heard someone cry out behind him and stopped immediately.

He turned and shock ran through him. "Dobson, are you all right?" he asked. She was on her back in the shallow water. He held out his hand to help her up.

She knocked it away. "I was just fine until I collided with your dog," she sputtered, glaring at him.

"He ran into you? Koda, bad dog. I'm so sorry." Heat crept up his neck.

"No, he didn't actually knock me over. But I didn't see him in my path. I ran into him."

"Geez, that's never happened before. I knew he was running behind me. I guess I got distracted." He felt like such an oaf. He quickly looked over Gray's dog for any damage. "He's fine."

"You should pay more attention to him if you're going to run through a populated area," she said, glaring.

Already he regretted running on the beach, but she didn't have to act so insulted. "Are you all right?" he repeated.

Dobson brushed the sand off her swimsuit and shot him a glance. She stopped in front of him and tilted her head up to look him in the eye. She just looked at him, saying nothing but staring into his eyes. Desperately, he aimed his at her face when he realized he'd been ogling her. Her slim shoulders evoked a strong sense of need. Her curves made his mouth go dry. Water droplets on her skin sparkled and transfixed him.

But he didn't want to be drawn in. Getting drawn into a woman's eyes meant a man was interested, and he definitely should not be interested.

But he was. Why were they having such a rough start to their relationship?

"Yes, I'm fine." She shielded her eyes from the sun as she looked up at him.

He could have hugged her right then and there. She'd rescued him, unknowingly, from numb tongue. The awkward moment when you get caught staring at a woman and no words fill in the blanks.

An edge to her voice said she was not fine at all, but Jasper ignored it. It was a little less sharp than her initial words.

"Good. Then your day at the beach won't be spoiled."

"No, it is not. Thank you," she said.

"For what?" He probably shouldn't tease her but he hated a meaningless thank you.

"For asking if I'm okay."

"Of course. I'm sorry you and Koda crashed into each other." The awkward was back. "Well, I'll just get back to running."

"Jasper, Jasper!"

He heard his name called and looked around for where it was coming from. He heard it again and saw two women approaching.

"Someone's calling your name," Dobson said and followed his line of sight. "Do you know those women?"

"Yes. They're sisters." He waved back. "Hi!" It was good to see friendly faces. And maybe, Dobson would drop the whole 'your-dog-knocked-me-over' thing.

Rachel and Cherish walked up and hugged him.

"What a nice surprise to run into you two," Jasper said.

"I'm not one bit surprised to see you on the beach, Jas." Cherish punched his arm teasingly. "Isn't it a lovely day?"

"We couldn't pass up spending a day like this at the beach." Rachel peered out onto the rolling waves.

Jasper cleared his throat. "Where are my manners? Rachel, Cherish, meet Dobson Ramirez. Dobson, meet Cherish and Rachel." He deliberately left off Rachel's last name to avoid a difficult moment. He didn't know if there would be animosity from the sisters.

"It's nice to meet you," Rachel said. "We're sisters."

"Oh, you're sisters. Now I understand." Dobson blew out soft sigh knowing these women were not two of Jasper's girlfriends.

"Did you think we were Jaspers former girlfriends?" Cherish chuckled. "I'm his sister-in-law and Rachel here is Jasper's oldest brother's girlfriend. I wouldn't want to be mistaken for his girlfriend. The last one was a real, well, I'll just say it was painful to watch Jasper in that relationship."

"You know, I'm standing right here and you're talking about me as though I were in another room somewhere." Jasper wanted to crawl under a big rock. Worse, he couldn't stop thinking about Dobson's reaction earlier. She was noticeably relieved to learn they were sisters and were in relationships.

"I'm new in town." Dobson held out her hand to each sister. "I don't know many people other than the officers at the Dunes Bay Police Department. That's where I work."

Cherish and Rachel exchanged a glance, then Cherish chuckled again. "We're lawyers. We recently opened our own firm. So we know many of those officers through our work."

Jasper noted Dobson started chewing on a fingernail. "Am I the only new person in town?" Her voice cracked, and he decided it was time to get Koda's attention and move on.

"You might be. But it's a friendly town, so your list of friends and acquaintances will grow." He slanted a smile. "This has been a real pleasure, but I better get this dog running again. Enjoy—"

"Dobson, would you like to join us on the beach?" Rachel interrupted. "We have plenty of room under an umbrella. It's right over there." She pointed to a yellow and blue beach umbrella.

"Oh, I don't want to intrude. I was just getting ready to leave when I ran into Jasper."

Jasper swallowed hard. The sisters had no idea Dobson was working with their parents, their criminal parents. He was unsure how any of them would react to that news, so he'd rather not interfere. They would have to handle that sticky situation themselves.

He bent down to pet Koda. "C'mon boy, let's finish our run. I'll see you all later."

"Oh no you don't." Cherish pulled on his arm, laughing. "You two have to tell us how you met."

Rachel rubbed her palms together rapidly. "Are you old friends?"

"No, no." Jasper forced himself to avoid Dobson's eyes. "We met at a mutual friends' wedding." He made a circle with his foot in the sand.

"Right. Jasper helped me find my seat at the reception." Dobson laughed lightly. "And I found his spot, which happened to be right beside me. We ran into each other here on the beach coincidently."

Jasper knew Rachel and Cherish well enough to know they were intuitive and could pick up on small cues, but Dobson was crushing her story. It was obvious to him she wasn't willingly going to reveal her connection with the sisters' parents. Not yet.

"Like I said, Koda and I have a date with a run."

"Yeah, I need to do some errands. It was lovely meeting you." Dobson nodded her head to each one of them, then walked briskly off to the beach parking lot.

"I don't know Jasper. She practically ran away from us." Rachel leaned her chin on her finger and sized him up.

"I thought so too. What are you hiding from us?" Cherish asked.

"You two are overly suspicious. Dobson and I really hit it off, that's all." He stared out at the lake for a couple silent seconds. "Well, it was nice seeing you, but I have to finish my run and get Koda back home."

Jasper ran like a bull was following him all the way down the beach for another two miles, then to his car. He dried off Koda before letting him in the car, his brain retracing the conversation with the women. Dobson had held her cool until the last minute. There was something wrong with their strategy of denial. It might come back to bite them, when Cherish and Rachel discover the connection, as they surely will.

* * *

DOBSON WALKED up the stairs to her apartment fuming.

It was stupid. She hadn't lied. But she should have told the two women who belonged to the Steele family that she had been mining their parents for information about the Espositos. She hadn't lied. But by not disclosing the relationship she would now have to own up and that was going to be so humiliating. Proof again that she had poor decision making skills. Her tombstone would be etched with, Dobson Ramirez lies here. She was known for her serial poor decision making.

She'd spent about thirty minutes lying on the beach and gotten restless. A quick wade in the water cooled her down. She'd strolled a ways on her way to the parking lot, enjoying the serenity of the lake when she'd plowed into the dog. Her gaze had been on shimmering water and not on where she was going.

Then Jasper was there. And she'd lost her cool. Highly overreacting out of embarrassment, she felt ashamed. It was happening too often. Why was her anger so quick?

No more, she declared to herself. Her demeanor here on out would be gracious, professional, and kind, if it killed her.

"Is that you, dear, just getting home?" her mother called from the living room.

"Yeah, Mom." Dobson walked in to find her mother resting on the couch. "I wish you would have come with me. The beach was wonderful and the weather was perfect." She plopped into an uphol-stered chair and sighed. "You would have loved it."

"Did you get done at work?"

"I got done what I planned. The lake time was a great refueler."

"I'm happy hearing you enjoyed it. My lake time is coming to a close," Cecilia said.

"Oh don't say that. Tomorrow we can go together. It will be fun."

Her mother didn't reply for a full two minutes and Dobson held her breath.

"Mom, are you okay?"

Her mother's eyes were closed, sending chills up and down Dobson's spine. She leaned closer. Cecilia opened her eyes. Her face was drawn and her eyes were sunken.

"Don't worry about me, sweetheart. I'm just tired."

"Me preocupo por ti. I worry all the time." Dobson stifled a sob. "Did you eat something after I left? Let me get you some water." Dobson's hand trembled as she set a glass of water on the end table. "Here you go. Drink this." Her heart dipped to watch her mother slowly sit up and pick up the glass. She shuddered. Slow down, stop killing my mom, her heart screamed. Damn lung cancer. It wasn't fair. She'd already lost one parent. How could her mother be dying?

She'd asked Dobson not to tell anyone about her cancer. Her mother shied away from pity. But the burden of her mother's impending death was weighing on her chest like an elephant. Fear of being all alone knotted in her throat.

She made a quick phone call to her counselor and was able to schedule an appointment for as soon as she could get there, even though it was Saturday afternoon. She counted her lucky stars.

Dobson splashed water on her face and entwined her hair into a braid that trailed down her back.

"Mom, I don't want to leave you alone again but I have an appointment. I won't be longer than an hour," she told her in parting.

Located in downtown Dunes Bay, her apartment was within walking distance of many things, including her new counselor's office. She and her mother had planned it that way so it would be easy for her mother to walk where she wanted to go. Dunes Bay was no Chicago, but the downtown vibe reminded her of her former home town.

She missed the busy sidewalks of Chicago. It was easy there to fade into the crowd. It was its own kind of haven. Until it wasn't.

She shoved open the door to her counselor's office and strode inside. No one sat at the front desk and the room was empty, so she sat in one of the cushy chairs and scanned the waiting room walls.

Plants sat in the window, and a diffuser sitting on a shelf gave off a rich scent of rain and freshly cut grass. It eased the anxiety chattering like a magpie in her brain.

Dr. Harper Blye can't help you. No one can change what has happened. Deal with it privately. What's done is done.

The same old messages played over and over.

"Hi Dobson. It's nice to see you," said the tall, pleasant woman.

"Thank you for seeing me on a Saturday. It's nice to see you," she lied. "No, Doctor Bly, that's not true. I hate coming here. But I had no choice."

"Let's go back to my office."

Dobson followed down a short hall and into the office with more comfy chairs. Words were falling away. Why had she felt so compelled to talk with this outsider?

"Have a seat," the counselor said, and gestured to the couch.

"Thanks. She sunk into the soft cushions and noticed her muscles were taut. She deliberately tried to relax them, but couldn't.

"Please, call me Harper, remember?" She sat across from Dobson, crossed her legs and tuned into Dobson. "You're angry today?"

Now it was her turn to talk and she just sat there. "My mind is blank," she said.

"Okay, how does that feel? Can you describe what a blank mind feels like?"

Harper leaned in and knitted her brow as though she were truly interested, just as Dobson had last week at her first appointment. Then she'd gone home and eaten a pint of pralines and cream ice cream.

But Harper deserved a chance to help her, even if Dobson's heart wasn't in it.

"When my mind is blank it's sometimes because I'm weary." Harper stared into Dobson's eyes.

"Yes, weary is a good description. I'm not sleepy, but I'm so tired of fighting to stay alive."

Harper nodded her head. "Can you say more?"

Dobson balled her fists. "I'm so sick of not knowing why my dad died, why my mom is dying. Why everything went so bad at my former job." She pounded the arm of the couch. "I want a do over." Tears trickled down her cheeks.

"Do you suppose your tears are telling you what your heart is holding quietly?"

"I don't know," Dobson whispered.

"There's no rush. Stay with your heart. Let it give you information." Harper's voice was gentle but urging.

"When my dad was killed, I remember standing with my mom at the gravesite watching the casket lower into the ground. I felt like my heart was breaking open and I would die of the sadness I felt."

"That must have been terrifying. Did anyone know what you were going through?"

"The pastor took me away from my mom and told me I would make her feel bad with my crying, so he asked me to stop. I felt ashamed and I froze. I didn't want to hurt my mom." Tears streamed down her face. "He told me death is a part of life and I should be happy my dad was in heaven."

Dobson couldn't control the shaking throughout her body. She couldn't stand the dark cloud in her chest. "I'm sorry I'm coming unglued, Harper," she said through it all.

"I bet you wish you could continue quietly holding together all your emotions and experiences of that time. But Dobson, you're doing a great thing. You're facing those harsh words and terrible reality and finding a way out. You're doing a good job. It's normal to feel overwhelmed by grief and loss. But you didn't get a chance to feel all that was there to feel. Now you're doing it." Harper handed her a box of tissues. "I'm sorry so much happened for you and that no one could help you. They didn't mean to do you harm but they couldn't manage their feelings and take care of you. Normal, but a tragedy for you."

"My mom took care of me." She couldn't bear to think ill of her mother.

"I'm sure she tried. But it was too big for her, too. She probably did her best. Unfortunately, a loved one's efforts are only good enough, not perfect. No one is perfect. We're all just human."

Dobson patted away her tears and let out a long sigh. "So am I cured?"

Harper laughed. "You tell me. You have spoken, and you expressed yourself eloquently. So is your brain connected to your heart now?"

"I'd like to try it out and let you know at my next appointment."

"I see what you did there," Harper chuckled. "Be sure to schedule it on your way out."

"Thank you, Harper. I feel like I can breathe."

"Good. Don't thank me. You did the work. You were very courageous. But let me tell you, inner work requires more than courage, though that is important. It requires time. If you keep working on your inner stuff, you'll feel better and better, but there are many, many layers of stuff to work on."

"Are you telling me I'm a mess?" Dobson squinted.

"I'm telling you you're human," Harper said. "And there is always more to learn about ourselves. It can be a fascinating ride or a lost potential. It's up to you."

CHAPTER 9

Jasper leaned against the deck railing at his house and stared out onto the lake. Clouds filled the sky and a brisk breeze off the water gave him goosebumps.

But he couldn't get his mind off Dobson. When Cherish and Rachel had joined him and Dobson at the lake, it was as if they were both on the same page without any prior discussion. It just happened. They worked as a silent team to throw off Cherish and Rachel from learning the truth about Dobson. He licked his lips.

It hadn't been the first time they were on the same page. He ran his fingers through his hair, remembering how their encounter had just happened, too. Jasper wasn't superstitious or a New Agey type of man, but it had to be a natural connection they had for some reason. *Hmm.* The matter was worth discussing with Dobson, if she would be interested in talking to him again. He'd ask her.

He glanced at his cell, then it dawned on him he didn't have Dobson's phone number. He started pacing across his living room. She'd been distraught yesterday at the beach. He couldn't help but wonder why, because she'd been so quickly angry about her run-in with Koda. Why was she on edge, he wondered. It was such a small thing, his curiosity for Dobson's wellbeing, but it drove him crazy. Urgency spread through him to talk with her.

He stopped mid-pace and remembered her temper and how he was disinterested in anyone coming into his life with a chip on their shoulder.

But, if he and Dobson shared a connection, well, that could be a rare and beautiful thing. Why would anyone ignore that possibility?

An idea bloomed in his brain and he quickly picked up his phone to call Coffee Easy. Perhaps he could persuade the barista to give him her phone number. If he had it.

Whoa, slow down Jasper. This is farfetched.

It would be better to call his friend Krista at the hospital. It was likely Dobson had left her number there in case Devin woke up.

Minutes later the nurse picked up her phone. "Hi Jasper. How are you?"

The happy hello from Krista gave him hope. "I'm good. You?"

"I'm ready to get my shift done, but I'm getting there. What's up? Let me guess. You want to know how Devin Raye is doing."

"Yes. Can I have an update?"

Her voice dropped lower. "He's not good. But you didn't hear this from me."

"Damn he's hanging on. Have you called Dobson?" He winced, feeling a little manipulative.

"I have not. It doesn't look good for her to get an opportunity to talk to him. I should have contacted her but work has been so hectic."

"I could call her for you. I want to talk to her anyway. Do you have her number?"

"If you don't mind. You being the EMT who brought him in. You got a pen?"

He wrote down her number and hung up, vowing to bring Krista a coffee for helping him out. He texted Dobson asking to take her to lunch, then he started pacing again. He made sure his cellphone's sound was on, and checked for a return text. Finally, he dropped his phone on the couch and resigned to let it go.

The sun would be high in the sky soon and he still had time on his day off for some fun. He checked the outside temperature on his watch and went for the keys to his jet ski. On his way to his bedroom he heard his cell ring and dashed back to the living room. "Hello," he said, his pulse racing.

"Hi, this is Dobson. What's up? I figured if you got a hold of my phone number somehow it must be important." The edge was back in her voice.

"You could say that. I have news of Devin and I also wanted to ask you to meet me at Darcy's Diner for lunch," he asked.

"I'm at home with my mom enjoying a pleasant Sunday morning brunch, but I suppose I could meet. How about one o'clock?"

"That works. I'll be the guy in the booth." His attempt at levity fell flat, but it was worth a try.

"Seriously? No rose?" she played along.

Jasper laughed. "I'll buy lunch."

"In that case, I'll see you there soon."

The call ended abruptly, but Jasper didn't care. He had a lunch date.

INSIDE THE DINER, Jasper glanced around for Tricia. She was his favorite waitress. When he spotted her he gestured toward the back booth and she nodded, grabbed some utensils and napkins and headed in that direction.

He smiled to himself. Could be she liked him, too. Of course, she did make tips.

He slipped into the booth just as Dobson walked through the door. From where he sat he caught the wave, the turning of heads her appearance elicited. It stirred his heart. In a Gray T and white shorts that fit her just right, she looked all summery and relaxed. He waved to get her attention.

"So, you brought your friend again, I see," Tricia said.

He nodded and looked up at Tricia. "Could we make this booth mine and it would always be open for me? That way I could tell Dobson it's my booth." He grinned at Tricia.

She rested her hand on her hip. "Trying to impress her, huh? I'll work on that," she joked. "Hi Dobson, he's been waiting for hours for you." She winked at Jasper.

"Liar," Jasper teased. "I've been here a few minutes."

"Who should I believe? The waitress who I'm sure would never lie, or you." Dobson pointed a finger at him.

"Don't let her fool you," Jasper added. "You can't trust a person who works for tips."

"Ha! I'll give you a few minutes." Tricia wove through tables on her way to the kitchen.

"You two know each other well, I see. That's nice to be able to walk into places and be recognized as a friend. I had that, too, in a few places when I lived in Chicago."

He hung on her words. He tried to imagine her predicament here in Dunes Bay and knowing no one. He started to feel bad for her, and time passed.

He suddenly noticed she was looking at him and startled back to the moment. "What did you say? Sorry, kind of left the planet for a few seconds, but I'm here now," he said, putting on a serious expression. I talked with the nurse from the ICU. She told me Devin is still in a coma and his chances of coming out of it in his present condition are slim. I'm sorry. He might not make it for you to talk with him."

"Damn," she exclaimed, frowning. "I could sure use his testimony to put more Esposito affiliates in jail for good, lengthen Teddy's sentence, and eliminate his entire network."

"Oh, that's all?" he cracked.

She faced him. "I don't mean to be anything other than professional."

"I understand that about you." He leaned his chin on his hand. "Could we change the subject?"

Dobson's lips tightened. "Of course. What do you want to talk about?"

"I was thinking, you're right, we jumped from A to D all in one evening. And now when we're together, we act like strangers. Is it too soon to ask, how do you see our *us* going forward?

"That's a lot to unpack. First, let me remind you we have no us. We have never been in a relationship," Dobson said.

Her eyes glittered with intensity. It was a different sort of passion and he wanted to know more. "I get your point. So you're saying there is no going forward with us."

Dobson sighed heavily. "Is that what you want?"

"Whoa, slow down. You're moving too fast for me. I did not say that. I want to know what you want. So you've said your first of all, what's second of all?"

"Second is that it's too soon to tell."

"You want your space. I get it." Jasper was reading between the lines. It was his defense, he knew.

"Only a little space," she said, and her eyes twinkled brightly. "I think we got a great start to a relationship. But, it was different, unique. We can't simply tread on to more sex and sleepovers. It has to make sense."

Jaspers heart raced. He liked her. He liked how her mind worked. She was complex and thoughtful and angry all wrapped up in one beautiful person. "I would like to get to know you better. We'll think this thing through."

"Yes, very intentionally. But spontaneously." Excitement shone on her face.

It was contagious. His brain felt alive and hope grew for something meaningful and fully engaged in which he wouldn't be invisible. Dare he take the risk of shattering disappointment?

"That day, before the wedding, I thought I was going to explode. Longing in me begged for spontaneity." Dobson paused for a moment. "I had been living in a box for so long and I wanted to stretch out of it. You didn't know that about me, but your invitation was exactly what I wanted."

"Is it a sign?" he teased.

"I believe in signposts along the way through our lives. I don't know that we're meant to be together. But maybe. Let's not jump ahead."

"We would never jump ahead," Jasper said, chuckling.

"Very funny. I haven't been looking for someone. Not at all."

"Nor have I. I've had casual relationships but nothing has ever lasted. I learned my lesson about what can go wrong with relationships with my last girlfriend."

"What was the lesson?" She leaned closer.

"Respect my own needs and values." A smile stretched across his body as the words came out. He didn't know the answer until she asked the question. "I'm trying to think positively about her and my experience and not just globally dismiss all possibilities love could be awesome." He grimaced. Thoughts told him to back out, not get too honest about his feelings.

Tricia walked up to their table bearing water glasses. "Have you decided what you want?"

"We have," Dobson said.

Tricia took their orders and left them to continue their probing conversation. Dobson tapped her fingers to the country western song playing. Jasper regarded her in silence, a little confused. She had listened, but would she truly hear him and go further into emotional stuff? He cringed at what he'd done. He'd blatantly laid himself open for ridicule. He pulled in, crossing his arms over his chest.

"You know," Dobson started. "I think those insights were potentially well worth the experience, despite the ugly stuff. Amazing that you have been able to embrace those insights."

She lowered her eyes and blushed.

"Thank you. I can't say I've always been happy about the experience of knowing that woman. I'm mostly glad that the relationship is in my rear mirror," he said.

Her gaze still lowered, Dobson wriggled in the seat. "I missed the moment I should have put certain things in my rear view mirror. Now it seems I can't."

Jasper froze. He hadn't expected her to reveal a private matter. But he didn't want to leave her hanging in the breeze. He slowed down his thoughts and looked inward for a helpful response. It mattered to him.

"We all probably go through something we regret because it turns out wrong, but do you mean you can't put it behind you?"

Just then Tricia arrived with their food. "Here's your adobe shrimp and roasted Brussel sprout tacos, Dobson. And the barbecue chicken grain bowl for you, Jasper. Do you want anything to drink other than water? I know you want water, Jas."

"Dobson?" he asked.

"Water would be great. Thank you."

Tricia left, and Dobson sighed. "I'm probably giving you too much information. I don't know why our conversations get deep." She put a finger to her chin. "You know, you're different from a lot of men. You're very curious and you like to dive into emotional stuff."

"I still would like to know your answer to my question."

She shook her head and took a bite of her taco.

CHAPTER 10

$\mathcal{J}$asper peered at her while she chewed. How did he do that, look straight into her soul and dare her to reveal her secrets?

The longer she chewed the more tender his look became. Question was, how long could she chew one bite?

Her heart softened. Maybe she dared to go to that dark place in her heart and let some light in. She swallowed and took a drink of water.

"You are persistent, too," she said. "Why do you want to know?"

"That's a great question to dodge answering. I'm interested in interesting people."

"You think I'm interesting? That sounds like a morbid peeping Tom."

He slanted his smile engagingly. "That sounds like a defense. But you know, I don't mean to push your buttons analyzing what makes you feel stuck. I just care when someone opens a doorway just enough to let me know there is an unspeakable problem."

Weariness of too much drama and fear in her life made her want to lay her head on his shoulder and rest. She locked eyes with him. "I had an affair with a married man. I didn't know he was married. I called off the relationship when I found out."

"The jerk. I'm sorry that happened to you, Dobson."

"There's more. He was involved with another cop stealing drugs from the evidence room and selling them through a network of dealers. I found out and reported it to my lieutenant." She got quiet. She'd said enough.

Jasper squinted his eyes. "I suppose that didn't end well for anyone."

"No, it didn't. One of the detectives killed himself with his own gun, the other one was forced to retire early. I moved to Dunes Bay to get away from constant harassment from my fellow cops. But, I'm getting anonymous phone calls. It might be someone from Chicago, maybe Wynne."

"He's the jerk who deceived you?"

"Yes. Whoever it is isn't saying anything but I can hear breathing. It could be someone Teddy assigned to intimidate me into dropping my investigation."

"So that's why you said earlier, Pick a name."

She nodded and looked away. "You can't make this up." Tears threatened to spill, but she refused to be in that helpless place.

"Can I help you?"

Jasper's gentle voice triggered more tears. "I haven't talked to anyone outside of Chicago about this. I don't want it to get in the way of my work. Please don't tell anyone else about all this." She took another bite of her taco.

"Of course not. I respect your privacy. But you don't have to go through this alone."

"I'm not getting you involved. It could be dangerous for you." Dobson chewed on her thumb nail.

"Let me please be there for you. Just tell me you'll keep me in the loop."

Dobson touched his hand. His skin was warm and comforting. Jasper's fingers folded over hers. He'd proven he noticed things, noticed things about her she hadn't told him. It gave her hope, or at least the promise of it.

"I've never had this happen before. I'm unsure what to do," she said.

"*This*? What is *this*?

"You, you're showing concern and interest in what I'm going through. It's not normal. People are caught up in their own lives. You have a life, it's a good life with family, work, and lots of fun. Can I trust you, truly trust you, Jasper?"

He dipped his head and she saw him trace a small pattern on the table. It made him real. He wasn't just all talk, he had feelings and angst of his own.

"You've touched my heart, Dobson. I haven't been through the things you've talked about, but I can imagine how devastating it would be. I hope to prove to you I'm trustworthy. If you need emotional support I can do that, because you deserve it."

"You seem to know what I'm thinking and feeling. Maybe it's a stretch to say we share a vibe, but it seems like it."

"Right?"

She withdrew her hand from his grasp. She squared him. "Listen, you should not get involved with me. I'm too much of a hot mess."

"It's too late. I am involved with you, hot mess or not. I like getting to know you. You're complex and I like complex people." He took her hand again and leaned closer. "Don't laugh. I think we have a connection. Remember when we both collaborated to keep your identity from Cherish and Rachel? And we did it earlier too. If I'm right, why wouldn't we take notice and see where things go?"

"Because you might get killed. I can't live with that." Her brow furrowed and her eyes pleaded with him. "I'll agree to more between us if you make a promise."

"Just any promise? I promise to finish my coffe—"

"No. I'll tell you what you must promise me. I mean this. You must promise not to get seriously hurt or die."

"I can't make a promise I may not be able to keep," he quickly said, and held up two fingers. "Scout's honor. I'll be careful."

"You were a Boy Scout?" Her surprise came out all over her, she was sure.

"No. Rhys was."

Dobson punched his arm. "I'm serious."

He melted right in front of her. "I'll do what I can to keep us both safe. I'll bring in the Cavalry if I have to."

"You know people in the Cavalry? Get out." She let a small smile escape at the corner of her lips.

"I'm referring to my brothers. We each have one another's backs."

"You're not taking me seriously," she said, frowning.

"I am. I've stepped up to the plate when Gray was in trouble with some bad cops, Chicago cops, at that. Again when Rhys was in deep danger with the Espositos. We can be downright lethal. Not that we've ever killed anyone." Jasper pursed his lips. "You know what I mean, right?"

"I'm getting the picture. The three of you are vigilantes."

"Stop turning everything into a bad thing," he grinned. "We have *brodar*. We understand each other as though we're one, but we're individuals. When one is in trouble, the others come help. It's what family does."

Dobson couldn't help but laugh. "It's cute that you are all are so loyal and take care of each other and have a name for it." That didn't come out how she intended and Jasper looked like he'd been slapped in the face. "It's sweet and very special. You're lucky to have brothers who are so dedicated to helping. I'm an only child. I always wanted a big brother and a twin sister."

"You can have mine." His face shone with compassion. "There are plenty of us to go around."

"Sure," she said and nodded her head. "You have to stop saying nice things. I might believe them, then I'll lose my way."

"You won't get lost. You know what you're doing."

Dobson laughed.

"Do you want to go for a walk? It's a nice summer afternoon."

"No, I need to get home. I haven't spent much time with my mom today. She lives with me. She's alone."

"It's great you can be together." He flashed a million-dollar smile. "Okay, I'll give you another rain check. Right now I can walk you to your car."

On the way out of the restaurant, Jasper grabbed Dobson's hand and waved good bye to Tricia. Out on the sidewalk the sun burned hot, but it felt good on her face. Despite the heavy conversation they'd had, joy flowed through her. The feel of his hand on hers was enticing.

"You're quiet," he said, as they strolled to her car parked on the street.

"So are you." She wanted to know what he was thinking. Was he replaying their conversation?

"I'm savoring this moment, in the sunshine, with you."

"Me, too." She stopped at a midnight blue Volkswagen beetle and leaned against it. "Thank you for lunch. It was interesting. I'm going to hold you to that raincheck."

He stepped closer and brought her hand up to his lips and kissed it. "Is that all right?" he asked.

Tingling in all the places in her body, she couldn't deny the kiss was enticing. "It's more than all right." She looked up into his eyes and smiled.

He moved another step and she felt his body against her.

"Then is this okay?" He tilted his head and touched his lips to hers, gently, sweetly.

Breathless, her head spun. This was so unexpected all things considered. But parts of her responded whole-heartedly.

Jasper stepped away, put a kiss to his fingers, and pressed his fingers to her mouth. This should have been a warning sign. She was losing control of old patterns that protected her.

But damn it! She didn't want to live confined inside those patterns any more.

Dobson placed her hands on each side of Jasper's head and kissed him hard.

CHAPTER 11

*A*n amazing coffee scent wafted in the air as Dobson walked just before eight in the morning into Coffee Easy and placed her order.

"Haven't I seen you in here a few times in the last couple of weeks?" asked the barista.

"I confess. I'm a coffee addict. I'm really enjoying your basic brew of the day, but I like to explore different kinds sometimes." The barista's smile and the welcoming atmosphere in the shop wrapped around her and gave a lift to the afternoon.

"My name is Andre."

"Nice to meet you, Andre. I'm Dobson. I'm new in town, so I appreciate your friendliness. This is my third Monday at my new job."

"Welcome to the community," he said, and handed her a pastry.

"What's this? I didn't order it."

"Consider it a welcoming treat." Andre took her payment and handed her the coffee.

"You're so sweet. Thank you. I'll see you around." Dobson had a thought, and turned back to Andre. "I'm going to introduce my mom to this place. She's a coffee lover and it would do her good to get out more. It seems like this would be a safe place for her."

"Sure. We have a number of elderly people visit us. She'd be welcomed to get to know us. We're open every day from seven in the morning to ten at night."

"That sounds perfect."

Outside, Dobson slipped behind the wheel of her Beetle and made the quick trip to the police station.

A couple of blocks from Coffee Easy she noticed a vehicle in her rearview mirror. It made the same turn she did closer to the station. As she pulled into the parking lot, she watched it slowly passing by. The windows were tinted too dark for her to see inside the vehicle, but it creeped her out.

The black SUV parked on the other side of the street a few buildings away. Frustration turned into anger. If Teddy wanted someone to keep tabs on her, he should appointment someone with more brains than the person hanging close to her.

She checked for her gun hooked on her belt, just to make sure, picked up her cell phone, and marched to the parked vehicle. She tapped on the window. "Open the window!" She could see the face of the man in the driver's seat. "I said, open the window!"

He failed to respond, so Dobson reached for her cellphone in her back pocket and pulled it out. She pressed 911 and held up the phone for the man to see. "Unless you open your window I'm calling the police." She stood solidly, glaring.

Seconds passed.

"I'm counting. When I reach three, I'm calling."

The window slowly rolled down. The man in the car looked to be in his forties, had black hair, and looked Latinex. Just like her but nothing like her. "Give Teddy a message for me. Make sure you listen."

"I don't know anyone named Teddy," the man said. His face was blank.

"I'm telling you, give him this message: If you want to talk to me, call me yourself. Got that?" she asked.

"I know no Teddy," he repeated.

"Just do it. As for you, stop tailing me. You're no good at it. Now go!" she ordered.

She stepped aside and he pulled away from the curb and headed down the street away from her.

She pivoted and walked to the department door, her muscles trembling. She'd put herself in front of a possible mob assassin. What was she thinking?

Inside, she strode to her office and dropped into her chair, resting her head in her hands. Geeze, Teddy was getting bolder. Getting more fearful, undoubtedly.

She crossed her arms over her body and tried to lower her anger. Ridding herself of fear was next, but right now she had to calm down. How dare Teddy put someone on her.

A knock at the door penetrated her thoughts, but just barely.

"Come in." She braced for an uncomfortable interruption.

"Hey, Dobson, do you have a minute to discuss your schedule? I can't find—"

"Not now, Tandy," she yelled.

"Are you okay?"

Dobson turned to her. "I'm angry. But not at you. I just need a minute."

Tandy backed out from her office and gently closed the door.

Working with criminals was part of the job, even mobsters at times, so she was used to being cautious and vigilant. But she had convinced herself she had Teddy where she wanted him, metaphorically speaking. Guess I was wrong.

Get on with it, she prodded herself. She rolled her shoulders, then dialed the number for FBI agent Zachary Young.

She held the receiver to her ear and counted the rings. Three. Four. Five.

"Agent Young, can I help you?"

"This is Detective Ramirez, Zach. I need to talk. Got a minute?"

"Hi, Dobson. I've got just about that." He chuckled. "What's up?"

"I visited Teddy over the weekend. I'm certain he ordered the hit on Devin Raye."

"Good work."

"Today someone followed me and parked outside the station. I confronted him and he left."

"It sounds like you scared Teddy and now he's coming after you. That's good and bad."

"I know. I succeeded in making him question his position, but in the process put myself in his crosshairs." Dobson pursed her lips, waiting for a response.

"Should I put agents on to protect you?" Zach asked.

"No, I know what's going on. Teddy wanted to scare me into backing off. He's not going to get what he wants, so I'll find out what comes next, but thanks for the offer."

"If we could tie Teddy directly to attempted murder, we could get his sentence lengthened."

"Right. He is cagey but I'll keep at him." Excitement at the possible outcome fluttered in her stomach.

"Dobson, are you all right? You're playing close to the edge. I'm sure it was upsetting to see an assassin tailing you."

"I'm fine. I was really angry, still am. I hate bullies." She chuckled, making light of the situation.

"Okay, good. Just don't make light of it. Teddy is out to get you and anyone around you he thinks would kill your soul," Zachary said, his tone serious.

"I know what he's capable of, and I'll keep that in mind."

"Good talking with you."

"I'll see you Friday at the meeting."

"Yup."

Tandy walked up to Dobson's desk. "Mr. and Mrs. Moss are waiting for you." She grimaced.

Dobson chuckled. "Thanks. They can be difficult." She went to the reception desk and winced. Adrian as usual looked perky but Emma scowled. "C'mon back."

They followed her to her desk and sat across from her.

"Thank you for coming in. I want to acknowledge your cooperation on the Teddy Esposito case. It's still open, but I'm not expecting to need you for anything further." She watched their expressions but nothing changed. "However, I need you to cautious, still, as the Espositos are actively exacting revenge. They caught Devin Raye skimming money and killed him."

Emma's hands flew to her mouth as she gasped. "Oh my god! Devin is dead?"

Adrian's eyes dropped and he took Emma's hand. "I'm sorry to hear this. He was a good friend." He turned to Emma. "That could have been us."

"I know." She squeezed his hand and sighed heavily.

"I'll still need you to be accessible if something comes up that you could help me with. But please be cautious, as I said. Do what your bodyguards tell you."

"We will. What about Cherish and Rachel? Are they in danger?" Emma asked.

"The potential is there. I've warned them to be aware of their surroundings." Dobson swallowed hard. The sisters had been thrust into a dangerous situation that had nothing to do with them.

"We'll see to it. We don't want anything happening to them." Emma said, wiping a tear from her cheek. "Is there anything else?"

"No," Dobson said, standing. "Take care of yourselves. If anything questionable arises please contact me."

"We will." Adrian assured her.

Dobson at back down, her mind shifting. She opened the Esposito file and scanned the info, looking for something that would help her get ahead of Teddy.

According to his criminal record, eleven-year-old Teddy and his thirteen-year-old-brother Marco were taken from his parents and put in the foster care system due to their drug addictions. Marco and Teddy had essentially been on their own up to that point, but had already been buying and distributing meth and oxi.

So, a bad start in life. He might have abandonment issues, she speculated. He could have been a wild kid, without parental love and support and joined the gang, probably looking for a place to belong when he was eleven, and his criminal life escalated.

Dobson knew all this. Bad start in life, poor choices looking for love and an identity, lost at nineteen, when he killed a man with a knife while in prison. In prison, out of prison, more crimes. His wasn't a unique story.

Teddy's brutality was written all over his record, but repeatedly he had protected his brother Marco and Marco's sons. Maybe that was the pressure point she needed. Threaten his family.

She'd figure it out. But she needed to protect her mom.

Thoughts of her father and his death pulled at her heart. She couldn't help thinking of how he'd been killed in a gang war on the streets of Chicago. As an agent in the FBI, he'd worked undercover. That's all she knew about his death.

Enough, she told herself. Those thoughts from the past would only bring down her spirits and get in the way of her present work.

An ambulance siren interrupted her thoughts as it drove by, delivering thoughts of Jasper.

A smile took her over as she imagined his intense blue eyes and playful demeanor. He'd been so kind to her and her own fears had pushed him out of serious contention.

She cleared her throat and returned to brainstorming how to cut off Teddy before he caused harm to her or her mother. That should be her priority now.

* * *

TAVIS FLEW by the police station in downtown Dunes Bay, weaving in and out of traffic on the way to an accident on old Route 66.

Jasper looked out the passenger's window to see DBPD windows, thinking of Dobson at work in her office. The building blurred by as the bus sped through town.

The rig tilted a bit on the turn. "Sorry about that," Tavis offered. "I really am in control of this thing. That turn crept up on me."

Jasper grimaced. "I know. Stuff happens."

Tavis laughed. "You know my policy about criticism. If you don't like my driving, you drive."

"I know," Jasper pointed. "There's our road right up ahead."

"Right." Tavis checked his watch. "We're about five minutes from the accident."

Jasper noted the time. He took the time to get ready for what they might find. He swallowed hard and clenched his teeth. Maybe what's up ahead wouldn't be tough to handle.

"Number twenty-two sixteen, what's your ETA?" asked 911 dispatch. "The situation is worsening. The vehicle is smoking and a child is trapped."

"Dispatch, we're almost on the scene."

"Truck number forty-two is ten minutes from scene," dispatch said.

As they arrived, Jasper jumped out of the rig door and ran with his medical kit to the car. He sucked in a gasp. Smoke was pouring from the front of the car and he could hear a young child screaming.

A woman ran up to him and pulled on his arm. "My son is trapped in my car. He's scared. Oh, I hope he's okay. Hurry, hurry!" she begged.

"What's your name, ma'am?"

"Suzanne. My son's name is Aaron. He's only three. Please help him."

"I will. I need to know if there are any other passengers in the vehicle."

She wrung her hands. "It was just me and Aaron. A truck hit me as I was going through the intersection and we rolled a couple times before we landed on the car roof."

"Thanks, Suzanne. You stay here and I'll get to work."

Jasper turned his attention to the vehicle. The firefighters would take care of the burning car, but it was his job to check on the people.

The sound of the boy crying sliced through him. There was time to get him out and back into his mother's arms, but not much. He lowered his helmet, and moved close to the car. It sat upright and was really banged up. Adrenaline burst through him.

"Aaron," he said to the little boy over his cries. "Hey, Aaron, I'm going to get you out of the car in just a few minutes." He gave the boy a thumbs up and smiled. "You're all right."

It was challenging ascertaining the boy's condition, since he was so young. But from what he could see, the child's car seat protected him from major injury and there was no blood of any significance.

Jasper moved swiftly to get help. "Tavis, right here. Bring the cutters now!" He hollered toward the bus. We can't wait for the firefighters to arrive."

The mother fell apart at the sign of the Jaws of Life and Jasper ran the few yards to her and ran off what he had to tell her. "Your son looks fine. I can't say for sure until I examine him, but I think he's okay. He's crying because he's afraid."

"Thank you, thank you. Just get him out, please," she cried.

"I'm working on it." He smiled the smile he didn't feel. Confident of his skills, he still worried about unforeseen explosions or something unexpected happening.

He ran back to the car and checked on the little boy again through the window. It wasn't smashed, but he still tried to connect with Aaron to ease his fears.

"You're going to be with your Mommy soon," he said.

Tavis carried the cutters right behind Jasper. "Let's fire these up," he said, and the jaws came to life.

Jasper grabbed them and began cutting into the door, very carefully. The front passenger seat had been jammed against Aaron's legs during the roll. "Damn it," he swore. He shouldn't have been so optimistic with the mother. He chalked it up to his eagerness to help her feel better, and meticulously walked the jaws through the dented door, while Tavis helped move the section already cut loose from the boy.

"We're almost done, Aaron, hang on," Tavis said, while the boy put his hands over his ears and slowed his crying. "This is probably at once terrifying and fascinating to this little kid."

Smoke filling the car's interior while the firefighters tried to extinguish the flames made it difficult to see well, but even so, he could hear the boy coughing and see the boy go limp. "We need to get the little boy out, like, now!" Jasper hollered, finishing the cutting and using the spreaders to open a doorway out for Aaron.

Jasper fumbled in the dark smoke to unbuckle the child from his car seat and released him into his open arms. "He's got pressure marks on his legs. We need to get him oxygenated," he said, racing toward the bus. He laid the boy on the ground and checked his vitals, while Tavis administered oxygen.

Jasper grabbed a board from the rig, slid it under Aaron's body, and secured him. "Let's load him and get him to the hospital. I'll drive. Dispatch, 2216 leaving the scene en route to ER."

Inside the back of the bus, Tavis hooked up the little boy to monitors and checked his oxygen levels. Jasper slid behind the wheel and tore out, full sirens screaming and heading to the hospital ER.

JASPER STRODE out of the ER to the waiting room and sat in a chair secluded behind a large plant. One could say he was just having a bad Monday. But he knew this pain from any day of the week, and it never got easier.

Aaron was going to be okay. But the emotions of his close call remained. Jasper let the chaos of the injured boy rumble through him, his head in his hands. Once again, he waited to hear news of an injured person he'd brought in to the ER. Energy drained from his body and he wanted to shout out his frustration.

Life and death always felt so close together whenever he administered care to a seriously ill or injured patient. Repeated encounters with violence and death had changed him. He wanted to help people but it had become such a heavy burden. His shoulders shook and tears fell to his feet. Too often the outcome bored a hole in his heart. He knew it was wrong for him to be so weak, but how much could he be expected to process?

He started to slip into memories, a flashback of when he'd let down everyone when he didn't stop his friend in high school Riley Phelps from driving drunk. He rubbed his forehead, trying to stop the flashback. Riley's crash was the first time he'd been face to face with the knowledge that life is fragile.

He lifted his head and wiped his face, checking for signs anyone had seen him fall apart. He couldn't tell any of his fellow EMTs about his true feelings. No one would understand. Even the counselor he talked to didn't truly understand. Hopelessness creeped into his gut and he just sat there on the fringe of the waiting room sinking.

He shifted in his seat. Maybe he didn't have to unload to get past his desperation. Maybe he could lighten his load in a completely different way. A way of focusing on things that were not dire.

He made quick calls to Rhys and Grayson and invited them over for dinner. He hung up from each, encouraged that the evening could be a happy time that would distract him from his reality.

But a part of him searched for something more and found it readily. He wanted to see Dobson.

He straightened his back and texted her. Simply thinking about seeing her lifted his mood.

Moments later he read her response.

Thank you for your invitation to dinner. I appreciate you including my mother. I'd love to meet you at your house and see your beach. Send me your address and I'll see you at six o'clock.

CHAPTER 12

*D*obson's GPS led her to Jasper's house and she pulled in to the driveway. She helped her mom out of the car and they walked up the few steps to the house.

"This is really nice," Cecilia said. "It looks like the deck surrounds the whole house." She touched the railing around the deck and ran her hand over it. "Even the railing is pretty."

Jasper popped his head out the back door. "Hi! I'm Jasper." He took Cecilia's hand and walked with her to the front of the deck where it came to point, just like the A-frame home. "Look out there. If you think the deck railing is nice, how about the view?"

"Breathtaking," she exclaimed.

Dobson stood off behind her mother and watched as she was moved by the beauty. How could she express to Jasper how much this meant to her? "The lake looks so serene. Of course, living in Chicago we had access to the same lake. The view was different with tall buildings behind us and lots of people going places, but this, this is enthralling in a different way."

"I agree," her mother breathed.

"I'm a lucky guy to have this house. I love it here. Would you like to see the house? All three floors?"

"I would. But I think I could do just two floors, ground floor and the second floor. That's a lot of climbing." Cecilia turned back toward the door and Jasper took her inside.

Dobson entered the house behind them and it warmed her heart immediately. "This is a surprise."

Jasper stopped half way up the stairs to the second floor. "How so?"

"Your house is a beach house. You're a guy. I didn't expect to see homey décor and cleanliness."

"Give me some credit, won't you? My parents didn't raise me to be a lazy bum," Jasper said, laughing to himself. "When I bought this house it had been neglected for a while. It deserved better than a sagging porch and few windows. I wanted to open it up and let in natural light and showcase beautiful sunsets. I made a haven for myself and one for those who come to visit."

Dobson wanted to know all about why he picked the soft, pale blue-greens for his color palette, but didn't interrupt his tour for her mom. Rather than tail them throughout, she took a seat at the island in the kitchen and let her gaze drift to the amazing view of the lake through the wall of windows.

Their footsteps sounded as they climbed to the second floor. She could hear her mother's quiet commenting but couldn't make it out. Her heart melted just a little, absorbing the ambiance of Jasper's home. Who was this guy?

"Dobson, you should have come with us. My words couldn't do justice in describing this perfect home," her mother cooed.

Jasper bowed. "I'm glad you like it. It was my pleasure to show you around. Please, take a seat in the living room while I begin preparing dinner."

"I'd like to try the swing out there," Cecilia said, pointing to the large porch swing hanging outside.

"Good choice, Cecilia. Take this door right here." Jasper opened a door hidden in a wall of windows on the left. "Make yourself at home."

As soon as her mother was settled on the swing, Dobson walked back in to the kitchen and brushed away tears before Jasper could see them. She sat on a stool across the island from where Jasper was slicing chunks of mango into a large bowl.

"Smells yummy." What kind of small talk was that? Was she really going to talk about fruit when there was so much stuff in her heart?

"Here, have a bite." Jasper offered her a piece of the fruit. "Good, huh? It's fresh."

He wiped his fingers and rounded the bar to sit beside her. Her skin prickled at his closeness and his earthy scent.

"I need to tell you something I should have told you already. But I didn't want to prompt you to run away," he said, his eyes lowered.

"You think I run away from things?" Her heart hammered.

"Well, if the circumstances are right, I think we all run to get away from difficult situations."

"That's fair," she muttered. Her throat was closing up, as she wondered what he was about to tell her.

He looked in to her face, his brow knitted. "Do you remember Cherish and Rachel?"

"Of course. I just met them." Her hands in her lap, she twirled her thumbs.

"Oh hell. They are the daughters of Emma and Adrian Moss."

The knot in Dobson's throat dropped into her gut. Words failed to form in her brain.

"W-W-Why would you think I would have to run from them?"

"You're working on their parents' case. I thought it would be awkward, maybe worse. But I'm glad if you're okay with them being in your space. They are coming over with my brothers for dinner with us."

"Here? Now? Tonight?" She had to get out of here. She really, really did.

But. It was painful, but she didn't leave. She sat there on the stool trembling for no good reason and felt her feelings—fear, aghast, destruction, insufficiency—rumble through her.

"Are you okay?" Jasper asked, eyeing her. "Can I do something? Okay, maybe I didn't think it through. At the time I invited you and the others, it seemed like a good idea to let you meet them up close in a casual atmosphere."

"Please don't do anything more." Dobson looked out toward the deck where her mother was singing to herself. "What about her? She knows about my work. Is this going to be uncomfortable?"

"She'll be fine with it. She's cool. It's not like I invited Emma and Adrian."

His eyes pleaded with her very gently, but his discomfort was palpable. Did she really need to make a fuss?

"I'm not leaving. I'm going to stay right here and be strong. I'm going to be downright friendly."

"Phew," he said, and let out a long breath. "Friend to friend, Dobson, I'm sorry. I didn't plan to run into Cherish and Rachel at the beach the other day. But when we did I didn't feel it was my place to tell them who you are, the lead detective on their parent's criminal case, though their part in it is over, right?"

"No. They are no longer in legal jeopardy, per se, but they are witnesses and if I have to apply harsh methods to keep their parents' cooperation I will." Strength coursed through her blood vessels. "There's nothing illegal about having a friendly relationship with their daughters. I can do this."

"Of course you can. If it matters, I'll be right by your side," Jasper promised.

"Thank you. I'll be fine." She slanted her head and grinned.

Jasper frowned. "I want to talk to you about us, more getting to know each other better." He glanced through the kitchen window at her mom.

"We can talk more. What do you want to say?" Dobson wondered how long this probing talking was going to go on.

The back door opened and a pile of people poured in, ending the opportunity to talk further. She straightened her shoulders and stood to greet them. All of them. They were loud, full of excitement, and, she had to admit, welcoming. But did Rachel and Cherish know who she was, what she was?

"Jasper, introduce your guest," said the man who introduced

himself as Rhys, Jasper's oldest brother. A definite similarity to the other two brothers made it certain he was a Steele brother.

"Everyone, this is Dobson Maria Perez Ramirez. Dobson, this is everyone." Jasper gestured to each one.

"Hey, that's not an introduction," said a young man in the group.

Jasper started pointing. "You've met Cherish. She is married to that guy right next to her. He's my big brother Grayson. The other guy is my oldest brother Rhys and his girlfriend Rachel, who you already met."

"It's nice to see you again, Dobson," Cherish said.

"Yes, for me, too. You don't have to use all those names. I'm just Dobson Ramirez. The whole list of names is traditional naming." Dobson stood in a semi-circle of Steeles and Mosses. Her fingers got cold and her nose started to drip, but she ignored her symptoms of flight or fight, hoping no one would notice.

Gray and Rhys stepped forward and offered handshakes.

"Happy to meet you," Rhys said, shaking his head. "How did you get mixed up with this dufus?"

"I'm Grayson, Gray for short. You must be new in town and already you two have gotten to know each other? How long have you been in Dunes Bay, Dobson," Gray asked.

"Just a bit more than two weeks," Dobson offered.

"Dobson's mother is out on the deck. Let's join her." Jasper herded them outside.

"Oh, my. Who are all these people, Dobson?" her mother asked, rising from the swing.

"Oh don't get up. Everyone—"

The group groaned, interrupting Jasper. "Not this again," Rhys said.

"It's the most efficient way of introducing you all. So, everyone, this is Cecilia Renee Perez Ramirez. Mrs. Ramirez, this is my family. The only ones missing are my parents. Now, everyone introduce yourself while I go check on dinner."

Dobson stayed at her mother's side, watching her warm up to the new friends. She ran her gaze over the water, the steady sound of waves slapping against the shoreline coaxing her to be optimistic about this family. That they enjoyed each other stood out clearly among them. It seemed at first glance to be the kind of family she'd always dreamed of having.

On his way to the kitchen, Jasper stepped up beside her and touched her shoulder. It sent shivers gliding through her.

"So, are you surviving meeting my family?" he asked. "They can be a handful, I know."

"They are a friendly lot. So far no one has asked what I do for a living."

"Don't worry. Someone will. They're giving you space to get comfortable."

Jasper's touch helped hold her feet to the ground. It was nice.

But it didn't mean anything special. With his knowledge about her life, Jasper could send her life spiraling. How had she allowed herself let down her walls?

"If so, I'll handle it as best I can," she said, trying to project a sense of power and strength.

His eyes held hers for a long minute. "Great. Then you're okay."

"I am." She gave him a smile.

"Right." He left her standing apart from the crowd and strolled into the kitchen. Dobson knew she should turn around but she didn't. She watched him walk away, and suddenly sadness enveloped her. Being left behind was such a familiar feeling, it reverberated in her heart painfully. She turned to her mother to check in.

"Would you like to go inside and cool down, Mom?" she asked. Her mother's face was shining from her eyes to her broad smile. She hadn't looked so engaged and happy for a long time.

"No, dear. I'm enjoying this beautiful evening on the lake. It brings back memories of my childhood years on Lake Michigan in Chicago." Cecilia breathed in a long pull and let it out slowly, leisurely.

"I'm happy, too."

Her mother shot a knowing look her way. "Jasper seems like a very nice young man. Are you two in a relationship?"

"Mom, no. We're not even dating. I met him on the job. He's an EMT."

"He saves lives, then. He's a hero. It would make me very happy to know you had someone like him in your life when I die…soon."

"Mom!" Dobson exclaimed under her breath. "I barely know him. And who says you're dying soon?"

Her mom placed her hand over Dobson's as they sat on the swing. "My doctor, sweetheart."

Stubborn tears threatened to spill down her face, but Dobson refused to let go. Her mom was young, only fifty-six, too young to die and leave her all alone.

Jasper walked out onto the deck, chopping knife in hand. "Could one of you please help me here?"

Dobson jumped up. "I will." She escaped to the kitchen with Jasper rather than sit there trying to explain her misty eyes.

"Thank you for helping me out," Jasper said.

"I'm impressed with your kitchen. It looks like a professional set-up, with your counter top grill, double ovens, and extra sink built into the island."

"I like its versatility. I cook and bake more interesting things beyond just basics," he said. He handed her a cutting board, a couple of green and red peppers, then surrendered his large chopping knife. "Please cut these. I'm comfortable working in the kitchen, but I'm a little overwhelmed with the fish. I need to prepare enough for everyone." He swiped at his brow.

"No problem. I can do other things in addition to cutting, if you need me to." Dobson went to work. "Do you want sliced or diced?"

He looked up from his fish. "Uh, diced. I could put some music on. Would you like that?"

"No, I'm enjoying the background sounds of conversations and lapping water."

"Mmm…two of my favorite sounds." He cracked a smile in her direction.

Their gazes hung mid-air for a flashing moment. "That's nice," she said, searching for something less troglodyte and more sophisticated. "Nature is very soothing."

"You like being in nature? I ask because you grew up in a big city." Jasper carried his pan of fish to the counter next to her.

"Yes, I have always sought out parks. That's nature." Dobson didn't have to look at him to know he was close. His closeness flowed through her like warm butter, coaxing her to accept. She stared at the vegetables she was working on, as though engrossed. She could hear his breathing and it brought him closer without taking a step.

"Dobson," Jasper said, his voice husky. "You've diced enough peppers." He put his hand over hers, preventing her from using the knife.

She looked down at her handiwork and saw a pile of diced peppers three inches high. She gasped. "Oh my." She turned her head to look into Jasper's eyes. They were dancing with delight, and then he dropped his lids for a brief moment.

In that moment she couldn't breathe. Longing for something she couldn't pinpoint heated her skin.

Jasper gracefully slid close, close enough to press his body against hers. Her heart fluttered, and she lifted her chin to meet his lips. He kissed her once, twice, and a third time, so softly it felt like a butterfly's touch, but so enticing she wrapped her arms around his neck and held him there.

Heavy footsteps penetrated her trance. She pulled away quickly from Jasper's arms and they exchanged a panicked look.

"Look like you're busy," Jasper whispered.

"Hey you two, how is dinner coming along?" Gray asked. "I'm getting hungry." He walked upstairs to the bathroom.

Dobson noticed Jasper swallow hard.

"Gray and Rhys have sensitive radars. I suspect Gray doesn't know what he interrupted but he probably picked up clues that something was happening," Jasper whispered in her ear while they were alone.

They worked silently side by side, waiting for Gray to return. Gray's footsteps on the stairs prompted a sideways glance at each other and a wink from Jasper that tickled her heart.

Gray took a seat at the isle and thumbed through the cookbook Rhys left open.

"You could speed things along by building a fire on the beach. The fish will be ready to grill by the time your blaze dies down," Jasper said.

"I can do that. But first I want to talk with Dobson," Gray persisted.

"What about?" she asked.

"Oh, don't encourage him. He's a journalist, so he likes to dig into things that aren't his business."

"Jasper. Stop. I mean you no harm," Gray told Dobson.

"I'd rather talk over dinner." She shot Gray an impassioned glance.

He nodded. "Okay. That makes sense. I'll make fire."

"Yeah. I'm starving."

Inside, Jasper sighed. "Sorry about that."

"For the interruption?" she asked. "We almost spilled the beans." She chuckled. "But we got lucky."

"You could say that. But it could be simply our odd predilection to get physical when risk of exposure is great." He shivered.

CHAPTER 13

The setting sun filled the sky with deep crimson, golden yellows, and vivid purple, giving the beach picnic a brilliant show. The fire had died down during dinner and now made perfect, squishy marshmallows for s'mores.

Just as Dobson licked melted marshmallow and gooey chocolate from her fingers, another couple walked up to the fire.

"Hi folks. What smells so good?"

Jasper jumped out of his beach chair to greet his mom and dad. "You made it, finally." He took the dish his mom carried and set it on the wooden table that held other food.

"You grilled your catch, right boys?" his dad asked.

"Grab some chairs and enjoy what's left of the meal," Gray urged.

"We knew you were coming later, but we didn't wait. We were hungry," Rhys added, both brothers rising to hug their parents.

"There's plenty left," Jasper said, offering them clean plates. "I cooked perch, sunfish, and Coho salmon that are still hot on the grill. Right there is grilled asparagus and there's a fruit bowl." He gestured to the different dishes, trying to make the two of them feel welcome.

Issues with his parents, particularly his mother, stirred under his skin, as usual, but he loved them, thanks in part to the fact they were wonderful people and also because he'd worked with a good counselor. Still, the marks from his experiences remained tender. A memory of a tough time popped up in the front of his brain and his gut squeezed. The memory was an old one of riding bikes with Rhys when he was twelve. It still made him shrink inside.

They'd taken off to explore new places in the neighborhood but Rhys fell when they tried to ride in gravel. Jasper remembered telling Rhys he would get help, but he couldn't find his way home. Finally, after biking around for a while, frantic, he had to go back to Rhys.

Boy you are such a dummy.

Rhys climbed on his bike, his leg bleeding. Follow me. I know the way.

The incident stayed with him and he hated himself even now. He'd learned he wasn't as smart as his brothers and that belief colored his whole life.

He came back to the present just in time to hear Gray guiding the conversation.

"Okay, let's have another round of this-is-my-name, glad-to-meet-you," Gray suggested. He pointed to Cherish and Rachel's parents. "You first."

"I'm Adrian Steele. I am father to Cherish and Rachel. It's nice to be here tonight. I am also husband to Emma. Your turn Emma."

"Why do we have to introduce ourselves? We know you all," Emma Moss whined.

"No, you don't," Dobson said. "My name is Dobson Ramirez and this is my mother Cecilia."

"You both have beautiful names," chimed in Rachel. "Dobson, where did your name come from?"

"My abuela. Dobson was my white grandmother's maiden name. I only say that as an explanation for my non-Latinex name. My father and my mother were both from Brazil."

"I'm these young men's father, Thomas Steele, and this is my wife——"

"I can introduce myself," their mother said. "I'm their mother and my name is Susan. I'm happy to join you all on this lovely evening."

Gray pointed a finger at his wife. "You next, babe."

"I'm Cherish, Gray's wife. Rachel here," she said, pointing, "is my sister and Rhys's friend."

"Thank you for introducing yourselves," Cecilia said, coughing and clearing her throat. "You have a very nice family. Cherish and Rachel, what is your last name?"

"Moss," said Rachel.

"I'm Cherish Moss Steele. We're very fortunate that both the Mosses and the Steeles all live in town so we can be close to both sides of the family."

Jasper stood very still, waiting for the truth to sink in. He stood like that for a couple minutes, then let out his breath. Why were he and Dobson so worried about telling the truth?

"Ramirez, Dobson, why does that sound familiar to me?" Rachel surveyed the group, looking as though she thought someone would give her the answer.

Everyone was silent, with only the sound of leaves in the trees around Jasper's house rustling in the warm breeze.

Then Rachel's eyes widened and her hand flew to her mouth. "You're the lead detective on our parent's case with the Esposito crime family. But…but…why are you here with Jasper? How do you know each other?"

"I met Jasper on the job," Dobson admitted, figuring Rachel forgot what she'd told her on the beach about meeting Jasper. "We didn't think about the case at all when we met. We ran into each other again at a wedding. It was coincidence and we're just friends." Why was she talking so fast?

"I see. I didn't put two and two together before now." Rachel exchanged a look with Cherish that Dobson couldn't read.

"This revelation will take time to process. I hope you understand," Cherish said.

"I do. I have no agenda for you or your sister." Dobson's defenses were quick to respond to the threat of broken feelings. "That goes for all of you. No harm no foul."

Despite all her good feelings earlier, Dobson withdrew inward and hung on the edges of conversation. She listened and nodded appropriately but her insides turned in turmoil. The little voice in her head reminded her once again that she didn't fit in, didn't belong. The voice belonged to a little girl inside her who found living and belonging mostly lonely after her father's murder.

Susan raised her hand.

"You don't have to raise your hand to talk, Mom. Just talk." Gray grinned.

"Oh you boys are always teasing me. I just wanted to ask, Dobson, can you tell us how you met Jasper on the job, please?" Susan put another bite of asparagus in her mouth.

Dobson cleared her throat. "Um, well, I drove up to investigate what I'd been told was a car accident a few miles outside of town and there was Jasper, leaning over the victim, delivering care."

"Oo, such a hero," teased Rhys.

"Shut up. My first reaction to Dobson was to yell at her."

"Let me guess," Tom said. "He didn't like your presence on the scene."

"That's putting it mildly." Dobson tried to boost the mood, rather than bring it down. "He told me to back off. He had patient care to do and I was interfering. And I was."

"He said that? That you were interfering? Jasper, be nice to the lead detective," Susan cautioned.

"Okay, okay. I admit I started out a little hot. But I apologized, didn't I?" He shared a certain look with Dobson.

"You did," she said. "And I'll admit that our interactions after that first meeting also were touchy."

"Did he continue to boss you around?" asked Cherish. "You are kind of bossy, Jas. But I still love you anyway." She blew him a playful kiss.

Jasper pretended to cry. "Stop bashing on me. How many times must I apologize?"

"Son, you should know better. Dobson seems like a nice person," Tom Steele said. "It's all in fun."

"I know. I know. I'm fine," Jasper said.

Cecilia stretched and yawned. "I'm sorry for being a wet blanket, but I believe I need to get home," she said. "It's getting late for me."

"Of course, Mom. We should go."

"But first I want to say, thank you for a tasty meal and a very nice evening." Cecilia leaned on her daughter to get out of the chair. "Good night everyone."

"I second that thank you. I had a nice time. Sleep well and I'll see you around." Dobson tried to leave things at that and started up the path to the deck.

"Wait a minute, you two." It was Rachel. "You're not disappearing into the night. I'll be in touch and the four of us women could meet for lunch soon. Is that okay?"

"Of course. Jasper has my phone number. You can call anytime."

"I meant it. I'd like to see you again, introduce you to Dunes Bay," Rachel said.

"I would too," said Cherish. "Lunch would be fun. We're both working women and we have a new office in the works. We could give you a tour."

"Of course," Dobson repeated. Confusion filled her head. How was she supposed to respond positively when she knew these women were not wild about her or her work?

Her phone rang in her pocket. "I'm sorry. I meant to mute the ringer." Her blood froze when she saw the caller's name, and she stepped to the edge of the group for privacy. "How did you get this number?" she demanded.

"I have ways of finding out anything I want. I want to talk with you," Marco Esposito said. "You can't hide from us."

"By us I gather you mean you and your fellow criminals?" Her fingers trembled as she recognized the danger everyone was in now.

"It's too early to know how far you'll make me go before you'll understand I'm serious. Don't forget your conversation with Teddy."

"Point taken." She disconnected and gathered her confidence.

"Who was that?" Cherish asked. "Whoever it was upset you."

"It was work. I just didn't expect to get called for work tonight." She didn't want to scare everyone but urgency to get them to safety burned insider her. "Wait, who am I kidding? That was Marco Esposito, Teddy's brother. Somehow they found my personal phone number. It's not safe here out in the open. I'm sorry. I probably shouldn't have come. Mom, we really need to go now. You all should go inside, too."

"Hold on," Gray said, his lips taught. "Why are these people threatening you? I thought all the Espositos were jailed."

"Not all. And besides, Teddy can run his business from inside prison." Dobson eyed her mother for signs of fear, but Cecilia looked calm.

"Holy shit," Rhys exclaimed. "You're not in this alone, Dobson, right brothers?"

"We're ready and able to protect you," Gray volunteered. "It's what we do."

Dobson's heart pounded. She had to get them to back off. "These aren't some two dollar crooks, they're at mob level. You could die. Please don't do anything."

"We've joined forces for me and Gray on separate emergencies to outwit crooked cops and the Esposito mob. We can do things cops can't. Let us help," Rhys pleaded.

"No. Please tell me you'll stay out of it." Dobson crossed her arms over her chest. "Promise." She looked over her shoulders and toward a boat passing by on the lake, feeling sick.

"Scouts honor," said Gray and Jasper, complete with the three-finger salute.

"Rhys," Dobson warned.

"Okay. Scouts honor."

"Don't joke around. You agreed too easily, but this is serious." Dobson took her mother's arm.

"We get it," Rhys admitted.

"Well now that that's settled, can we all get off this beach before anything serious happens?" Cecilia said.

"I second that, Cecilia," Rachel said, picking up dishes and garbage.

"I'll help," Jasper said, folding the table and stepping toward his house. "I've dealt with both the dirty cops and the mob and I do not need to do it again. But Dobson, I will."

* * *

Jasper lay in bed, his mind whirling with the evening's conversations. He'd enjoyed the relaxed setting and the interesting interactions. But it had gone south for him before Dobson got the phone call. He'd noted a mood change in her at the point she'd revealed her name and her occupation. He was helpless to protect her from defensive reactions in the family, but they hadn't been harsh, only cautious.

He rolled over and tried to empty his mind.

It wasn't his responsibility to keep Dobson happy. Why did it matter to him?

He rolled back the other way and checked the time. The clock on his bedside table announced he wasn't getting much sleep tonight despite rising in time to start his six o'clock morning shift yesterday. Or was that today? On a sleepless night, what differentiates yesterday from today?

He couldn't feel worse for not asking Dobson for a real date, not one with all the family around that made a gauntlet for her.

He checked the clock again, then slid back under the covers and tossed one over his head.

His eyes closed, he breathed in slowly, then let it out deliberately. He sucked in another breath and exhaled. Sadness crept into his gut. It swelled inside his throat and he couldn't breathe. It was too early to call his counselor, so he was on his own.

He threw off the covers and let in the dark night. It weighed him down and he still struggled to breathe. Rogue memories of the insults his brothers and his sister-in-law threw at him twisted his insides. They didn't mean anything hurtful. It was teasing. The badgering was meant in fun not to hurt him.

Anxiety seared his heart. Just as it had when he went through it as the baby brother. It had made him feel less than his brothers.

He tossed and turned while lying unprotected from his memories in the dark. Everyone relied on his easy-going manner to hold things together, especially his mom. But that only meant he was supposed to take the bashing and stay invisible.

No one like Dobson would be interested in a guy who remains blank. "Someone who is always up for a good time but never says anything worthwhile. He loved his family unequivocally, but what about him? What about his self-loathing? Did anyone care?

It seemed like he had always, always been trying to keep up with his brothers. They were smart, talented, and confident. Rhys had proven his muster as a former coast guard and now as the CEO of his own business. Gray proved himself a brilliant journalist in Chicago and skilled Boatwright when he took over the family business. What had Jasper done but enjoy life?

He rolled over again and smashed his pillow under his head and neck, trying to get comfortable. The rhythm of the waves rolling into shore set a pace for his breathing. Thoughts slowed. His breathing deepened.

"The firetruck is coming, Miss. I'll stay here with you," Jasper shouted over the flames licking out from under the hood, trying to consume the vehicle. It looked as though the driver had lost control and the car had rolled down a sharp drop and landed upside down on the side of a hill. Heat from the fire was hotter than a kiln but he tried to get close enough to remove the woman in the driver's seat. In his full gear, the heat didn't place him in much danger, but the threat of the car exploding rose exponentially with every second.

Tavis was still up by the road in the truck, gathering supplies.

"Tavis, Tavis," Jasper yelled. "Come down here stat!

Tavis in his full gear was a big man, but he ran down the side of the hill in good time without losing his step. He ran up to stand beside Jasper and held up a pair of scissors. "I brought these. We can cut her seatbelt and catch her before she hits the car or the ground," he suggested.

"You read my mind." Jasper grabbed the scissors and cautiously pulled open the door. He charged on as he saw flames coming through into the interior near where the woman's feet hung. "You're almost out," he said, trying to calm the terrified woman. "What's your name? I'm Jasper."

"I'm Ginger," she managed to say softly, coughing and wheezing.

"Nice to meet you, Ginger . I'm going to cut your seat belt. I think when we cut it you'll be released."

"My seat belt is jammed." She coughed again, and went limp.

Time was too precious to talk any more. He heard the sirens blaring from the fire truck arriving up on the road, and breathed a sigh when he saw three firefighters approaching with a fire hose.

"There are fluids running from the engine down to the ground. We'll put out the fire, you get her out!" commanded the fire chief.

While water spray misted his face shield, Jasper worked on cutting the belt holding the woman in place and Tavis positioned himself to catch her.

"Oh, no," Jasper hollered. "I dropped the scissors. They're slippery." He and Tavis scrounged around the leaves and debris under the car to find the scissors.

"The fire is in the engine. We need to back out, you all hear me? Get out," the chief ordered.

Jasper stood up. "I can't find the scissors. I've got to do something!"

The fire chief grabbed his shoulders. "Get up top. Now!"

"But the woman, I can't leave her," Jasper hollered and pulled away. He shook her, trying to rouse her, but she didn't respond.

"No, no! No time. Get out now, I said. It looks like she's gone. We'll come back as soon as it's safe."

Jasper struggled to get to the woman, but the captain dragged him away.

"It's going to blow, get back!" called another firefighter.

Helpless to rescue the woman from the smoke-engorged car, he sank to the ground.

Jasper hollered and sat up, his eyes flashing open. He tried to gather his senses and tried to figure out why it was so dark, why he could breathe easily, considering a second ago there had been smoke everywhere.

He sank back down against his pillow and remembered.

Ginger's fate had been sealed when he'd dropped the scissors. Her death was his fault. The investigation into the matter had found him not guilty of reckless homicide or failure to act. But that hadn't changed anything for him. He'd hated himself ever since that day.

Ginger rode along with him in his mind on every call, cautioning him not to let go of another person.

Overwhelm pushed him out of bed and he headed to the bedroom window. He opened it wide and sucked in the fresh air to escape the nightmare. His heart pounded and panic rose in his chest.

"It's in the past. Let it go, Jasper," he said out loud, pounding his fist against the wall.

He could never move on. His work day after day reminded him of the dire results of making a mistake and all he could do was keep doing his best, crossing his fingers at the same time.

Well, not all. Jasper straightened his shoulders and grabbed his phone to check his calendar. He could talk to doctor Egan. It was too early to call the receptionist but he promised himself he'd call today. He wanted to heal and become whole, fully engaged in life for his family and friends.

CHAPTER 14

*I*t was time to talk to her mother.

Dobson stood under the shower head savoring the warm spray of water on the back of her neck. She poured shampoo in her hands and rubbed it in her hair, but a large portion of her attention was drawn inward. The family beach gathering last night left her with a strange mix of feelings: jealousy for the close relationships between the sisters and the brothers; and shame for her jealousy.

But above all else, aching to belong to someone she could enjoy a meaningful relationship with. Maybe more than one person. Maybe a group of people.

A darkness made her suck in her breath. She'd thought she had that in Chicago but it had backfired so badly she didn't know if she could ever trust anyone that way again.

She stood under the spray, her hands against the front wall of the shower for support, and cried silently. She thought of him, Wynne, the man she'd loved.

No, no, no. I'm not going to let him take me down again.

She rubbed her entire body dry, adjusting her mood to meet the present day. Enough of the past.

She dressed in a dark suit and crisp white shirt, paired with heels, and walked to the kitchen.

"Good morning," she said to her mother, who was already eating breakfast.

"I fixed you scrambled eggs," Cecilia said. "If you eat them now they'll still be warm."

Dobson sat at the table and took a bite of the eggs. "Thanks, these are good. You must be feeling better if you have enough strength to stand at the stove and cook."

"I'm content. I get to serve my daughter a warm breakfast and live in this nice condo. Yes, I'm grateful for everything I have and that makes me happy. Like this pleasant Tuesday morning."

"It's so good to hear. You mean so much to me, Mom." She finished her breakfast and gave her mom a hug. "Last night was fun, don't you think?"

"Well, I enjoyed the meal and the company, but I don't like that things got dangerous. It scares me that your work puts you in that position."

Dobson swallowed hard and sat back down. "I wanted to talk with you about that. I'm as safe as I can be. My work is important to me. I fight for justice, which means I put myself in jeopardy if it means I'll put criminals where they belong. Don't worry about me. Last night I was concerned about everyone, not myself. I was primarily worried about something happening to you."

Birds chirping outside the window contrasted greatly to the heavy subject of conversation. She wished so hard that her mother could just relax and get better.

"I understand your work is important. But if I could swaddle you in bubble wrap and keep you safe I would. You know that." Her mother's voice was firm. "Please take all precautions you can. I don't want to lose another family member to gun violence." Her face melted into sadness.

Her mother's plea and sorrowful expression brought up close that both of them were affected by her father's death. Even though he was killed so many years ago, emotions remained painful.

"Now don't fuss over me," her mom said. "Be safe. Que tengas un buen dia."

"I will have a good day. You too."

Dobson stepped out into the sunshine and warm air and decided to walk the six blocks to her work. As dreary as her morning began, she determined to smile at people walking by and stay in the present.

At the police department, she spoke with several officers and poured a cup of coffee from the department coffee maker.

She winced at her fist sip.

"I saw that," said her assistant Tandy. "Is this your first time trying our coffee?"

"Yes, I have to admit I'm taken with the coffee at Coffee Easy."

"Ours is an acquired taste. Don't give up on it. It's bitter, but it will wake you up and cure whatever ails you."

"Okay, good to know," Dobson said, walking toward her office wishing she'd stopped by Coffee Easy.

"I put your mail on your desk," Tandy said and turned toward her desk.

"Thank you." Her skin prickled at the idea of mail that could hold unexpected content from someone who hated her.

The pleasant feeling that had boosted her morning faltered. She sighed, knowing she had to accept that tough things were part of the job.

She tried another sip of the coffee.

"Oh, I see you're drinking the house coffee," the chief said. "See, didn't I tell you it's good?"

"I brought my own cup. Does that make me officially part of the team?" she teased. If she could protect his feelings and not lie about the coffee she would do better.

"It is official," Chief Neirling added, and closed her office door. "Say, I took a message for you earlier. I have to tell you your gunshot victim didn't make it."

"Devin died?" she exclaimed. "The hospital called and told you he'd passed?"

"Yes. I know you were hoping to interview him." He rubbed his chin thoughtfully.

"Bad luck, I guess." Dobson shivered. Welcome to square one.

"I'm sorry. Chin up," he said.

"Good advice. I have other contacts I can use. But it would have been sweet to be able to connect the hit on Devin to Teddy."

The chief tapped his signature beat on her desk and stood. "Good luck, Dobson."

"I'm taking all the luck I can get," she said under her breath.

She stared at her computer screen for several minutes, brainstorming where she could find another way to Teddy. She opened a file containing a list of known associates and scanned it. No one stood out to her. Frustration boiled. Ineptness crept to the forefront.

She shook it out of her head, unwilling to let it run her in the wrong direction.

"Drat. I don't need another distraction," she said to herself.

The unopened mail on her desk stared at her. "Oh frack." She picked up a plain envelope with only her name on it. It was strange looking without a stamp. She sniffed. It didn't smell weird so she tore it open. Stunned, she couldn't move. She stared at the Polaroid photo inside the envelope of her walking into the front door at the DBPD building. "Tandy," she called. "Who delivered this one without a stamp?"

Tandy walked to Dobson's desk. "It was a man who said the note was for you. He said it was urgent. Is there a problem?"

"I don't know yet." She jumped up and ran outside, hunting the surrounding area for a familiar face.

Her heart rammed hard inside her body and she couldn't catch her breath. He'd found her. She knew it. Shaken, she had to collect herself and go back to work.

How could she? No indications fingered him for taking the picture but she knew it was the work of Wynne. Wynne Doyle. One of the reasons she left Chicago, because things had gone so bad. The death threats from other anonymous officers had been scary enough. But

Wynne had gone missing. If she was right, he was here in Dunes Bay now.

Chills ran up and down her spine. So much for starting a new life. "Dobson."

The sound of her name brought her back. She looked around and saw Jasper walking toward her. Parts of her started crumbling and she tried to keep it together. The last thing she wanted was to spill emotions all over him.

"Hey," she called. "What are you up to?"

He ignored her question and marched up to her, narrowing his focus on her face. "Are you all right? You look, ah, troubled."

"I'm okay. What are you doing here? Aren't you supposed to be working your shift now?"

"I asked for time off. I need a break from doom and gloom," Jasper said. "But, I want to know about you. And don't try your distraction tactic. I'm on to you. Whoa, are you crying?"

"No." She swiped at the tears she couldn't stop from drifting down her cheeks.

He slanted his head. "Yes you are." He wiped a tear with his finger. "Here's the proof."

"I'm fine. I'm really angry, so don't mistake my tears for fear or sorrow." She heard the crisp tone of her words and regretted unleashing her anger on Jasper.

He opened his arms wide. "C 'mere."

Dobson didn't budge. How could she accept his hug and not fall apart? But he didn't wait for her compliance. He wrapped both arms around her shoulders and pressed her head against his warm chest. Loneliness dragged on her heart, but Jasper's tenderness soothed her.

She relaxed into his embrace. "I'm sorry," she said. "I shouldn't be doing this."

"What are you apologizing for?" he asked. "You're my friend. You don't need to apologize for having feelings."

He caressed her hair and she remained leaning against him. How long would she need this in order to walk back inside and go about her business?

She breathed long breaths in and out and pushed away. "You're so kind, Jasper. Thank you. I'm okay."

He nodded. "Sure you are."

She watched closely, drawn to the sound of his thumb scraping over the stubble on his chin. "I'm just having a moment."

"What happened to upset you?" His gaze softened.

"Nothing," she lied, and looked away.

Jasper sat down on the large, stone, flower planter on the edge of the sidewalk. "I know something happened. Why don't you tell me the truth, Dobson?

"I am fine," she repeated. "No matter how many times you ask, I'm going to say the same thing. I am fine." Why wasn't she telling the truth?

He held her gaze. "You can be honest with me. Just between us."

She slumped beside him. "You don't know what it's like. For whatever reason, my defenses come up without provocation. I don't always make a conscious decision to share personal information."

"I get that. Your self-protecting mode happens automatically. I do know what that's like. I do it too, to protect from being misjudged or made fun of, even in a playful way. I'm no counselor, but it seems like our coping mechanisms aren't doing a good job." He nudged her with his shoulder, playfully.

"I'll come clean if you will," Dobson said, her skin prickling.

"Deal." He offered his hand.

She grabbed it and shook it vigorously. "I told you I left Chicago PD because I wanted a change of scenery. There was more to it. I just didn't want to talk about it."

"Do you want to tell me about it now?"

She passed him the photo still in her hand. "This was on my desk this morning."

He gave her a serious look. "This is you outside the station. You look unaware that someone was watching you, is that right?"

"You're right, I didn't know. It has no context but I can guess the person who took it was giving me a message." She cringed inside. "This is hard, Jasper."

"You're doing fine. What's the message?"

He smiled. His encouragement meant she could go on.

"That the man, Wynne Doyle, knows where to find me. I've been hiding in Dunes Bay. Wynne is a former boyfriend who failed to tell me he was married."

"Jerk," Jasper exclaimed. "Why did you have to hide from him and what does he want?"

Dobson picked a blossom from the planter and fiddled with it. Her throat wanted to close up and stop her from spilling the whole sordid story. She looked around the plaza between the police station and the firehouse on the other side and yearned for a life do-over. "I wish our affair had never happened. When I broke up with him, he was upset. He didn't want me to leave but he also wanted me to pay for turning in two dirty cops who were stealing drugs confiscated in drug busts. One of them was Wynne. The other shot himself rather than face what he'd done wrong. Wynne was fired, he called it early retirement. It could have been much worse for him if the department hadn't decided to go easy on him. He did some prison time but not much."

"What? Why? Cops protecting cops?"

"I guess. The whole department blamed me for, quote, ratting on fellow officers."

"That's messed up. What a terrible experience," Jasper said. "What can I do?"

"Nothing. I am going to have to face the consequences of my actions. It's not fair, though. I wanted a fresh start, but now I'm looking over my shoulder all the time and wondering when Wynne will come after me wherever I go. He made that clear. I don't know what he'll do next." Dobson sighed heavily.

"Look, I have an idea. Like I said, I've got time off. Would you like to stay at my house for the rest of today and tonight? The weather is hot. You could cool off in the lake, lounge on my deck, or just read a book lying on the couch with the air on. Tonight we could visit Rhys's lighthouse, the best place on earth to view the night sky."

"I need to work," she said automatically.

"Right. But it sounds like you could use a carefree break. I'm just talking about a one day and night get-away."

"I can't just leave my mom like that."

"Can't you? She stays alone in your condo every time you go to work. To me, she looks capable and self-sufficient. I'd say bring her along but then it wouldn't be a break for you."

Jasper was winning this discussion. Could she take a mini-break? "You make some sense. I could go back to work tomorrow refreshed."

"With a rested mind you could find a break in the Esposito case," Jasper said. He looked over his right shoulder and his left shoulder. "Do you see that Wynne guy right now?"

Dobson scanned the plaza again and didn't see any signs of Wynne. "No, and I don't see any signs of Marco or another of the Espositos I know."

"That's good. I have to work at Gray's business, but I'll make it brief. Let's get you out of sight at my place. Do I get a yes?" He lifted his eyebrows.

"Yes. But I have to get some things at home first. It won't take me long and I'll be able to tell my mom that I'll be at your house."

"If I know your mom even just a little bit I'd bet she'll be happy with you tucked away someplace safe with me," he chuckled.

Dobson was sure about that, remembering her mother's suggestion that she date Jasper.

CHAPTER 15

*J*asper let himself in to Steele Boat Repair and Boatwright and surveyed the large room. One of Gray's projects hung from the ceiling. The room smelled of wood shavings and waterproof sealant. The partially completed boat hull hung in the room like ribs of a human body.

The work here was simple and felt more like chores, but he was happy to do them. The tradition and integrity of the business was something that gave the physical building a sense of warmth and honor.

Jasper went to work sweeping up piles of shavings on the floor and dusting it off everything. When he was finished, he worked on a small boat motor for a fishing boat and got it back to working order.

"Hey Jas, good to see you. You've cleaned up this place right well. Thanks."

It was Gray. "Somebody has to clean it." Jasper laughed.

"How did Mom take your phone call about missing dinner?" Gray slipped on his painting apron and tied it behind him.

"As you would expect. I am probably never going to tell her it hurts me when she carries on like she does."

"I get that. It's risky for your relationship with her, but whatever you must do for yourself, I'm behind you."

"Really?"

"Of course. I know the family gives you a hard time but I want what's best for you." He began applying sealant to the outer ribs of the wooden boat.

"How would you feel if I quit my job?"

Gray rested his paintbrush against the tray of sealant and sat down on an old beat up chair. "What's going on with you, Jasper?"

Jasper sat on a small barrel of seaming compound. He held his head in his hands and tried to find a way to explain. "I think my reasons for becoming an EMT were solid. Dad's heart attack was the second time I faced the reality of death. The first time was with Riley. I was so hurt by those incidents that I wanted to do all I could to prevent deaths."

"I get it. What's the *but*?" Gray poured them both a cup of coffee and handed one to Jasper.

"I have been instrumental in saving many people from dying. But, I witness a lot of suffering. It's been getting me down. Especially since the woman in the traffic accident died. That was brutal. I can't shake any of the gore, the gloom, the doom any more."

"So you've been thinking about a different line of work."

"I have. But I don't want to quit, on the one hand. I also, on the other hand, don't know if I can stomach the work anymore." Jasper ran his fingers through his hair. "I don't want to let anyone down. And what would I do. I need to work, of course. I'm not trained for anything else. If I quit, I would immediately be out of any kind of work that pays enough to support me."

"It's a real dilemma. I'd like to be the guy who could tell you what to do and be right about my advice. I'm not that guy." Gray sipped his coffee, thoughtfully. "Maybe you're simply highly sensitive."

"What does that mean?"

"It means your system—hearing, touch, taste, emotions—could be overloaded because you have the ability to use information from your environment that others can't. I think I see that in you. You use the information you pick up to make choices. But you also would get overwhelmed easier until you learn to manage your sensitivity."

"Boy, that was a mouthful. Do you really think I'm highly sensitive?"

"I can see it. So it would help you work with patients and pick up things that maybe other EMTs wouldn't. I think it would be an asset, but one you'd need to manage."

"Sounds complicated, but that would explain some things. Like, noise bothers me. I'm really sensitive to pain. I don't like spicy things." Jasper laughed. "This explains a lot. How did you know this?"

"I ran across an article about it in the Chicago newspaper. It's kind of a new discovery. Does knowing that about yourself help?"

"If I can find a way to manage it, I think it would. I would know that perhaps someone's screams for help amp me up and make situations feel direr than they really are," Jasper said. "You sent this work dilemma in a whole new direction."

"Hm, I was trying to help. When you said facing Dad's death opened your eyes to the fragility of life, I remember the article and that it said highly sensitive people feel deeply, more so than people who don't have that trait."

"True. The same thing could be applicable to how I react to Mom and her need for me to take care of her," Jasper said. He bent his head and in his mind's eye came an image of the wreck Riley caused so many years ago. A rock dropped in his gut and shame overloaded him. "I think there's something more. The shame and guilt over letting Riley drive that night is awful. I've carried it around, letting it drive me to find redemption for my mistake." His heart pounded in his chest as he stayed present with the guilt and desire to make amends.

"You're taking it too hard." Gray patted his back. "Have you talked to Riley about it?"

"I haven't talked to Riley for years. I kind of resent him for letting me take the blame." Jasper wiped sweat from his brow. "But we were just kids at that time."

"Exactly. Maybe talk with Riley. He might have felt guilty too. You made your amends already. Give yourself a break."

"Yeah, maybe. That would account for why he hasn't gotten in touch me either."

"I'm no psychiatrist but it makes sense." Gray stood up and grabbed his brush. "I'm proud of you, Jasper. You've had to deal with a lot of scary and dire situations in your life. You don't need to fix other people's problems, not even Mom's and Dad's. Just believe that they can take care of themselves." Gray smacked him in the shoulder. "There is nothing wrong with you."

"Well there is with you. You are obsessed with other people's boats," Jasper kidded. "When are you going to build me a boat?"

Gray eyed him. "When are you going to commission me for a boat?"

"About the time you tell me you'll do it for free."

JASPER HURRIED home to clean his house as much as he could before Dobson arrived. He sprinted through the house, sweeping, cleaning the bathroom, and tidying his kitchen and living room. He checked on his second bedroom, just to make sure it was ready for company. He wanted everything just right for her. Her story of how life had treated her resonated with him. With no agenda other than giving her a place to rest, Jasper's nerves still fired. She was so sensitive, so raw, he couldn't misstep or she'd be gone.

He worried about her life, though, just as much as her need for rest. What could he do to protect her? He could ask his brothers for help keeping an eye out for threats, but the idea of putting them in jeopardy didn't make him feel any better. Besides, they were working.

He had a thought, and quickly called Jordan Graves.

"Hey Jas, what's up?" Jordan answered.

"I need a favor and I know this is last minute, but it's important," Jasper said. "I want to hire you for the day to keep watch over Dobson."

"Really?"

"Yes." Jasper gave him the details and stressed the need for being discreet. "Could you do that?"

"Certainly. It's my day off. I'd gladly look over her today. You won't even know I'm around."

That settled, he sighed with relief. Now he could give Dobson a day to enjoy.

He was upstairs when he heard her at the door.

"Jasper, it's me, Dobson. Are you here?"

He ran down the stairs to find her at the open door, her hands full.

"Here, let me take your things. I'll put them upstairs in the bedroom left of the hallway. Please make yourself at home."

"Okay, thanks," she said, pivoting toward the living room.

"I'll be just a minute." Upstairs he took a minute to relax and make one more check of the bathrooms, then he headed back downstairs to her sitting stiffly on the couch.

"This is a very nice home, Jasper." She smiled at him. "I'm jealous."

He laughed. "Who wouldn't be? I sometimes can't believe I live here, right where I want to be, close to Lake Michigan. So, let's not waste a minute of our time. Would you like to take a book and sit on the deck or on the beach? Or would you rather go swimming, alone or with me? There's also a jet ski I could loan you."

"Loan me?" her eye flashed wide. "Drive it myself? I've never even been on a jet ski."

"Okay, so that's a no on the jet ski." Jasper enjoyed watching her expressions. Her face practically glowed.

"Relaxing on the beach sounds perfect, but I don't know if it's a good idea, under the circumstances."

"I thought of that. I've called a guy who works part time as a body guard. He's going to keep watch. You know him."

"Okay. That was good thinking. Who is this guy?"

"Jordan Gray."

"Yes, I know Jordan. Well then, where do I change?"

"Second floor, the room is to the left of the stairs."

Dobson took one step up the stairs, but stopped. "This is going to be great, Jasper. Thank you for your offer. I'll feel more in the mood for fun after I get protection set up for my mom. I should have done it earlier."

"I'm glad you can take advantage of my beach," he said and meant it. Feelings that made him cringe floated freely inside him. He wondered if he was taking advantage of a woman at her worst by bringing her into his realm. He gritted his teeth, watching her climb upstairs, and knowing he sincerely wanted to give her a break for her mental health. Was it her beauty that attracted him or was it her intellect and her spark?

He shrugged. For the time being, he'd be careful with her and not think too much about it.

Puttering around the kitchen, he checked his watch and looked upstairs. It was almost noon, so he needed to think about lunch.

"Okay, I'm ready to hit the beach," Dobson said, her face all lit up. She stood beside him in the kitchen. "You're not dressed. I mean you're not wearing swim trunks. Aren't you joining me outside?"

"Uh, do you want me to? I thought I would let you have peace and serenity, without me hanging around."

"Suit yourself. I'm going out to relax on the beach. Come join me if you feel like some sunshine." She grabbed her things, walked out the deck door, and headed to the beach.

Jasper watched her all the way to the point she spread out her blanket and laid down. His muscles tensed and perched between caution and the hell with it. Thinking he should hold back and give her space at the same time knowing the woman had invited him? He must be out of his mind.

He ran up the stairs taking them two at a time, driven by desire to be near her. In his bedroom he pulled on his trunks and snatched a beach towel. He almost tripped over his feet running down the stairs. At the bottom, he paused, slowing himself down. If he seemed too eager Dobson might get the feeling he was only interested in having sex, what with both of them nearly naked.

He took a moment to gather some food for the beach and some beverages. It was noon, not nine at night, so he stuck with water and lemonade in a cooler. Double checking everything, he pocketed sunscreen and picked up a beach umbrella, then made quick work of closing the space between them.

He stood above her on the beach as she breathed in and out softly. He refrained from waking her, understanding her fatigue, and let his gaze move over her. A warm blush rose to his face, even though he'd already seen her naked. Her tanned skin contrasted with her white swimsuit, her dark pink lips brought back memories, and her long black hair haloed around her head. Lying there so peacefully, Dobson could have been a fairytale princess. *And what, I could be her prince? Get a grip.*

He quietly put his things at the end of the blanket and situated himself on it. He stretched his legs out in front of him and propped himself with his hands behind him. The beach was quiet, except for the natural sounds around him. His pulse slowly calmed and he filled his senses with the touch of fresh air blowing in a breeze off the lake, the rustling leaves on trees, and his toes in the warm sand. He hadn't been this still in a while and it felt good.

Later in the day, speedboats would be roaring out on the lake pulling skiers behind. But right now it was as though he was alone in a sanctuary with Dobson. *Life could be just like this*, he thought, a smile lifting the corners of his mouth. It'd been a while since he contemplated something so seriously.

Suddenly, Dobson's phone rang beside her and her lids flew open. "Oh my gosh, I was sleeping," she exclaimed, picking up her phone.

"Do you have to answer it?" Jasper asked, hope in his heart for the reverie to continue.

She hesitated a nanosecond, then answered it. "Mom, what's up?" Her voice shook a little.

"You just got another threatening phone call. I thought you should know. I'm sorry to disturb you, sweetie." Her voice shook.

"I'm glad you called. Tell me about the phone call."

Jasper waited, tapping his fingers on his leg while Dobson's mother got her up to speed. Dobson's eyes narrowed and her lips tightened as she listened.

"These people are playing dirty," she said into the phone. "Don't worry about me. I'll see you soon. Yes. I'm having a great time."

She ended the call and tossed her phone on the blanket.

"So, bad news?" he asked.

She dropped to the ground and laid back, staring up at the sky. "How can something so beautiful like this beach stand alongside something evil, like Marco Esposito?"

"What happened?"

"Marco said to tell me I better be more careful who I go to the beach with unless I don't care about them, and threatened to come for her next." A sob escaped her lips, but her hands fisted. "He called her specifically just to tell me he knows how to hurt me." She pounded the sand and hollered. "Aaahhh!"

"I've been on the sidelines of the goings on with the Mosses and the Espositos, but from my point of view, the bad guys are wreaking havoc on the Moss family's lives. I think they're due for a downfall, the Espositos I mean."

"Thank you for that." She rolled to her side and rested on her elbow facing him. "The threats aren't going to work. I'm going to make sure of that. The Mosses have hired bodyguards, so they're safe. I worry about their daughters and you guys. The Steele family has been hit too. I know about Rhys's kidnapping."

Jasper meant what he said, but his mind was distracted by the swells of Dobson's breasts and the tightness of her abs. She didn't know that he was just as disappointed as she about the day being interrupted.

"I hate leaving my mother alone. I need to call Hector at the station and have him set up protection now. I don't think he'll go for covering you, your brothers, and your sisters-in-law."

"I don't need it and either do my brothers." He stared at her.

"What?" Dobson asked.

"I was worried about you so I hired an officer to keep an eye out today for someone stalking you. I thought it was necessary."

She said nothing for a minute.

"I don't care what you say, I felt it was important for your safety." He sifted sand through his fingers and waited for her to digest what he'd told her.

"I want to say thank you. But I don't need someone looking after me. Someone creeping around while we're having a day together."

"See? I knew you'd say that. That is why I didn't talk to you about it first."

"I'd really like to salvage this day. I need this day for refreshing."

"I hesitate to say, that's the spirit. It may be better to get you back to the police department where you'll be safe."

"No. Is your offer still good to ride your jet ski?"

"I don't know. I think my idea now is better. I wouldn't want either of the two threatening forces to hurt you." He wanted to give her the day he'd promised but his gut said abandon the plan. "How about we eat lunch and think about what to do?" He unloaded sandwiches, grapes, and dip with carrots from a basket onto the blanket.

"Okay, lunch first," she agreed.

They chatted lightly while downing lunch. Jasper stayed away from any deep or scary topics, just to save the peace between them. Foreboding in his stomach kept him from chowing down. He didn't know how he would do it, but determination to protect her hardened his muscles.

As they drank the last drops of lemonade, he loaded the bottles of water into his backpack along with their towels. His blanket wasn't needed so he ran it up to the kitchen and picked up his jet ski keys.

Back on the beach, Dobson, with her back to him, cast a slight shadow from the afternoon sun. She leaned on one long leg and rested her hands on her slim hips. He could have walked up behind her and put his arms around her without thinking twice. The scent of her clean skin still filled his head and he wanted to stick his nose in her hair and take in her sweet scent again. How did these emotions come on so quickly? It had only been a few days since he met her, and already he couldn't get her out of his head.

She turned around and waved him on. "Are you coming?" she asked.

He jogged to her, bracing himself for possible conflict. "Any second thoughts about jet skiing?" he asked.

Dobson waved him off. "I'm not letting Wynne or Teddy tell me what to do. They have no right and they're bluffing."

"Is that what your common sense says?"

"It's what my gut says. Listen, I hear the concern in your suggestion and I don't blame you. But if I'm to do my job right, I can't go into hiding. I don't want to, either. So, shall I find another way to get out on the lake or will you take me?"

Boy she was stubborn. If she was going to go out, he wanted to be there to protect her. "Yes, I'll take you. Not because you win, but because I don't want you out on the lake alone. Not now."

She slanted her head and gave him a coquettish smile. "Is that the only reason you want to go with me?"

He couldn't help himself. Her expression erased his sober face and he broke into a smile. "What other reason would there be?"

* * *

STROLLING along beside Jasper at the point where the water met the beach, Dobson shielded her eyes from the sun. The sunlight sparkled on the water, making a beautiful, undulating scene. Her body swaying on the wet sand, moved closer to Jasper and away again, like the waves on the beach. Everything was in motion in one gigantic synchronicity. She felt a part of the world and was grounded to the earth in a most pleasant way.

She gazed up at Jasper's face. It confirmed he was deep in thought, which accounted for his silence. Since she'd only known him to be talkative, she suspected he wasn't happy about their plans.

"You're quiet," she said.

"Hmm, so are you," he countered. "Is there something on your mind?"

"Nope. What's on your mind?"

He laughed. "I'm thinking about what we might run into out there," he said, gesturing to the lake. "The weather report promises sunny skies and low winds. But one thing about Lake Michigan is that conditions can change in a breath."

"I've heard that. Are you telling the truth? Is the weather really in your head? Or is there more?"

"Like what?" Jasper stared up ahead toward the dock area where his jet ski was docked.

"Troubling thoughts about danger and the threats coming true." She turned to face him. "Tell me the truth."

"I don't want to alarm you. I'm worried. But were I truly afraid for our lives I wouldn't have agreed."

"Cool. Let's change the topic. Where are we going to go?"

"I have a place in mind. I'm sure you're going to like it. First I'm going to give you a ride you won't forget."

His eyes gleamed with mischief, making her heart dance. She rubbed her hands together. "I can't wait. Are we almost there?"

"See that marina," he asked, pointing. "That's where we're going. It's only a short walk now."

"Faster if we run." Dobson suddenly sprang away. "Catch up!"

"You want a race, I see." Jasper chased her until he caught up to her, then he matched her pace and ran beside her. "This is a good speed," he said.

She laughed. "I bet it won't even make you breathe heavy."

"I'm fine with this pace," he added. "I wasn't expecting to run this afternoon. I thought we'd have a leisurely walk."

"Surprise! Spontaneity is refreshing. Besides, I could use a good run to deal with stress." She dared to wink at him, eliciting a big smile from him.

"Indeed."

As they ran up to the marina, excitement fluttered in Dobson's body. Boats in one area and jet skis in another bobbed alongside the long deck.

"By the way, Gray lives there," Jasper said, pointing to the building next to the marina. "He lives next door to the family business. Steele Boat Repair and Boatwright."

"I thought he worked as a journalist and manages the Dunes Bay Gazette."

"That's right. He worked as an investigative reporter for a big

Chicago newspaper. He took over the business when my father had a heart attack a few years ago. He owns the local newspaper and still writes on occasion for the big city newspaper. I help him out at the family business, doing things like repairing small engines and cleaning up the place. He makes a mess when he's sanding wood. But his boat repairs and constructions are masterpieces."

"Really. I'm sure Gray is thankful for your help." Dobson marveled at the members of Jasper's family. One gets sick and the others step up to take care of things. Another's schedule gets very full and another one helps out.

Jasper talked with some people she didn't know close by while she stood on the dock several minutes switching from one foot to the other, back and forth, impatient to get on the water. She was determined to hold the thought that it was going to be an adventure, not a colossal mistake. All she had to do was ride in back of Jasper. He would do all the driving. Thoughts of Teddy or Wynne lingered, but she shoved them to the back of her mind.

Jasper gave her instructions on how to stay on the jet ski and stay balanced, then handed her a flotation device. Finally, Jasper swung his leg over the seat and beckoned to her. "Your turn. Just climb on behind me and hold on here," he said, pointing out the rear hold handles. "Or you can hang on to me or my flotation device. I'm going to start out slowly, but I have to maintain some speed in order to prevent falling over. After we've started, if you need to tell me something, you can tap my shoulder or yell in my ear."

She stepped into the seat and searched with her hands for the handles and gripped them tightly. Her pulse raced, pushed partly by nerves and partly by anticipation.

"Are you ready?" he asked.

"Ready!"

He glanced around, looking for danger, but everywhere was just like any other day. Slowly he took off from the dock and drove out of the marina area into the lake. Then he steadily picked up speed.

The wind picked up her hair and blew it in front of her face as they tore through the water. The jet ski rocked up and down as it bucked against the rolling waves, and she quickly wrapped her arms around Jasper's lean middle.

"You okay?" he called over his shoulder.

"Yes," she yelled over the sound of the motor and crashing waves. "I'm loving it."

Water sprayed up and back from where the jet ski skimmed the surface.

Exhilaration ran through her, filling her lungs with full breaths of air, and expanding her idea of fun.

Jasper turned his head to see her. "Are you ready to take things up a notch?" A smile stretched across Jasper's face.

"I sure am," she called.

He made a wide circle once, then turned around to make an opposite circle. He'd told her how to lean with him at times like this, so she followed his lead to keep from falling off. Leaning and accepting the curve felt natural, like she was one with the experience. Her heart leapt, as though it had just started in her chest like a new born baby's.

"I didn't know I was missing this."

Jasper nodded his head. "That's the way with risk-taking. It opens your eyes to the pleasure of adrenaline boosts. You can't ever go back."

He slowed a little and pointed the jet ski closer to land and amazed her with the mansions built up on high points above beaches. It was hard to imagine ever living in such luxury but it was fascinating to see the opulence. She had no aspirations to live lavishly, but it didn't hurt to look.

Jasper took them up the shore to a place where there were no houses and where the water looked shallower. She dropped her hands into her lap and he turned around.

"Would you like to drive?"

"Where are you going? This wasn't mentioned before." Panic streamed through her.

"I can ride behind you or you could leave me on the beach here. It's up to you. I'm sure you'll do great. The way you moved with the changes in the water tells me you're a natural."

"What if I leave you on the beach and something happens while

I'm away from you?" In other words, what if he lied about her being able to drive herself? But why would he? Besides, she thought, a lot of people, men and women, have been known to drive jet skis. Why wouldn't she be able to do it?

Jasper squinted, his gaze aimed on the water. "Nothing bad will happen. But, if you drive it right here and up along where we saw the mansions, you would be within shouting distance."

Dobson ran her fingers through her hair, considering the worst that could happen. She might fall off. Wynne might show up. Marco might shoot her from a distance.

"I'll do it. I'll drive this beast, without you."

"Cool. The worst that could happen is one of the two people who have threatened to hurt you might come out of nowhere. That is highly unlikely." He dropped into the water and held the jet ski still.

She lifted herself onto the front seat and grabbed hold of the handlebars. "Here I go."

"Are you all right? Your face looks grim."

"I'm scared. But I am not going to miss out on this opportunity to experience joy just because of a bit of fear. Or a lot of fear."

"Way to go. I'll have eyes pinned on you the whole time," Jasper assured her, and let go of the seat.

She twisted the accelerator slowly. At least she didn't have to back up thanks to Jasper getting the machine in the direction she wanted to go. Another slight twist on the accelerator and the jet ski took off faster, leaving a wake.

Another twist and she was speeding along the lake where the houses on the hill stood majestically. But she didn't dare look for long. She needed to keep her mind on being watchful and focused. She didn't want to run into a boat just because she wasn't paying attention.

The water shoes she was wearing had plenty of grip to keep her feet solid on the footrests. A sense of power streamed through her, boosting her confidence.

She gave the accelerator another hard twist and felt the result of power taking the jet ski up into the waves and hammering back down.

"Woohoo!" she hollered, hoping Jasper saw her mini-jump and heard her excitement.

Nothing in her wanted to stop, so she rode a bit farther away from him. She could do this! And this was fun! Euphoria emptied her brain of sorrow and fear.

She leaned into the jet ski and cautiously turned it around. She waved at Jasper farther down the beach, still standing where she left him. So far he hadn't been wrong. She could drive a jet ski and stay on, plus no harm done by anyone lurking in the shrubs away from shore.

She slowed as she drove closer to Jasper, then cut the engine. She climbed off and waited for Jasper by the jet ski where the water was deep.

"That was the best ride ever. Thank so much for trusting me to go off on my own. I love it!" She threaded her fingers through her hair, trying to tame it. She couldn't contain all the good feelings and jumped up to put her arms around Jasper's neck and kissed him hard.

"I think you should take another drive. I like the results," he said, beaming. "It was all you. Like I said, you're a natural." He pressed a sweet kiss to her lips.

Dobson's heart couldn't have been fuller. She could fill her lungs, rather than take small, shallow breaths. She could dance around in the water and not feel ashamed for acting foolish. She could come out of the shadows because as long as she had her own power, she was safe. Now to make sure her mother would be safe when she brought her back home.

CHAPTER 16

"Before we get rid of the jet ski, I want to drive by Rhys's house. It's not far from the marina, just down the beach a ways from Gray's house. Then we should get you home before you freeze. I can see you shaking, and I know the temperature is cooling." Jasper rubbed her arms briefly before they got back on the jet ski.

"I'm fine."

"Okay, still, we're going back to my place soon."

On the way he drove faster, more confident about Dobson on the back.

Jasper was well aware of Dobson's soft skin as she laid against him, for warmth, he guessed. But the kiss she'd given him was still in the front of his brain, reminding him how good it felt to touch her, feel her, taste her. Memories of his former girlfriend surfaced and he tried not to compare her to Dobson. Olivia was too busy being angry to be very soft and cuddly. He doubted she truly loved him, but wanted to use him as arm candy. He knew that was true because in one of her rages she'd told him that was all he meant to her.

He pulled himself out of the memories. Hope for a meaningful, mutually satisfying relationship had helped him walk away from the dysfunctional one. Maybe, that kind of relationship could be had with Dobson.

Just then, Dobson pounded on his shoulder. "Look at that. It's gorgeous. Is that Rhys's lighthouse?"

"It is. She's a beauty, isn't she?" Jasper said. "I want to take you up top later if you're willing."

"Willing, honored," she said. "Would Rhys mind?"

"No. He's proud of that baby. We're going back to my place to shower and dress, then we can head over to the lighthouse. Actually, he asked us to dinner, but I didn't know if you'd want to. It might be too soon to meet with that crowd again. What do you think?"

"Could we play it by ear? I'm a little reticent after what happened last time."

"Sure. We'll see how things go. No pressure," Jasper promised. He pulled the jet ski beside the dock and Dobson climbed off.

She watched him dock the jet ski at the marina. He did it effortlessly, as though it was a muscle memory. Goosebumps scattered on her arms at the art of it. He immediately grabbed her hand and pulled her up on the dock. "Thank you for that experience, Jasper."

His gaze pinned hers but neither moved closer. "I had a great time. But there is more to do."

"Really? I'm just basking in the glow of this day's pleasure," she said. "Nothing could improve this day."

"Excuse me, I need to talk with you two." It was Jordan from the police department.

He startled her but Jasper didn't look surprised.

"Hey Jordan, that's okay. What's up?" Jasper said.

"I wanted to report to you that one guy was watching you at the marina. I tried to detain him but with the crowd all around he got away. He wouldn't give me his name or explain what he was doing. He had a gun. I could ID him if you have a picture. He had sort of sandy hair, about five-foot-eleven, white. Sorry, I tried."

"My god!" Dobson exclaimed. "It sounds like Wynne. He was practically in on top of us. He could have grabbed one of us. Don't apologize. Thank you for intervening."

"Thanks, buddy. I appreciate your help." Jasper shook Jordan's hand.

"I'm happy to help. But I don't know if I'll sleep well knowing that guy is still out there."

"I understand that. We'll be on the lookout." Jasper nodded and eyed Dobson. "You take care, okay?"

"You bet." Jordan nodded back at Jasper and walked away.

"So that was what we'd expected." Dobson looked over one shoulder and then the other. She looked up at Jasper. "Jordan could have saved our lives."

"Yeah, let's get out of here." Jasper took Dobson's hand and they walked to his house in quiet conversation about their options with Wynne, her mother, and Teddy. Eventually it turned to the weather, their families, and their lives. Nervousness trembled insider her. All of the danger and drama only made her more determined to make it all go away.

"Well, we're here. Just enough time to get ready and walk to Rhys's place," Jasper said. "Unless you don't want to go. I'm going to take care of you, Dobson. But if you'd rather go home or stay here, I understand."

Something between her and Jasper kept them standing in the kitchen facing each other. So many thoughts circled in her brain that she didn't know what to say.

"Going to Rhys's would be fun. Thanks for asking. I can't wait to shower off the sand and lake water and put on dry clothes," she said. In a flimsy cover-up, Dobson suddenly felt self-conscious like she hadn't all day in her bikini. Her whole body buzzed and warmth crept into her face.

"You can get in the shower first," Jasper said, looking away. "I have to fix hamburger patties for a crowd."

"I can help you. That's quite a few hamburgers."

"Thanks, but you don't have to do that. Feel free to get cleaned up. It won't take me long to jump in the shower and dress."

"Okay, I won't be long either," Dobson said, and went upstairs to the guest bedroom. She closed the door and leaned against it, releasing shivers and flutters to travel through her. If she had more time she would have liked to crawl under the covers to let the weight of the blankets soothe her jitters over the day's activities and the upcoming evening with family.

She stripped off her bikini and stepped into the shower. A strange sense of intimacy surrounded her being naked in Jasper's house. She moved deliberately, soaping her skin, then sudsing her hair. The spray from the showerhead warmed her through and through. She rinsed off then paused, imagining Jasper downstairs in the kitchen below her room. He'd already proven he was a good cook and handy around the kitchen. She chewed her lower lip, savoring the idea they were apart but close. Her eyes closed as she tried to put his sensual body out of her mind and she stood in the shower a little longer. This was a feeling she didn't want to hurry.

His whistling came up from the kitchen and startled her back into reality. Quickly grabbing a towel and stepping out onto the bathroom rug, Dobson hurried to comb out her hair and pulled on the shorts and sleeveless top she'd brought. A quick last glance in the mirror and she sat on the bed. What was she doing, falling for Jasper? She had to admit flirting with him a little and letting down her guard had been fun. But she couldn't be reckless. She'd already done that with Wynne and it had ended horribly with her fellow officers turning on her. What kind of 'terrible' waited for her if she made another error in judgement?

* * *

Jasper leaned against the countertop and held his breath. He'd practically lost it when he heard the water in the shower above him upstairs, letting himself imagine water dripping off Dobson and her skin all shiny in the shower.

He ran his hand over his lips and tried to set aside desire. Longing to be seen for who he was thudded in his chest. He wondered, could it be you?

She had the beauty part down pat, but she also was a complex and interesting woman. He could see himself falling hard for her if she would let him. Would he take the risk? Risk was his middle name. But could this attraction be the riskiest thing yet? Would she disappear him, reject him, devastate him?

He moved items around in his refrigerator to make room for the burgers and ran upstairs to change. They passed in the hallway and his nostrils filled with lemon and clean linen scent. It was an oddly tantalizing mix. "You-You are ready. You beat me by a long shot." He was so taken aback that he stumbled on the first two words.

"You had to make a lot of burgers," she said, laughing. "I won't leave yet for Rhys's house, I'll wait for you," she joked, taking him off guard.

"Appreciate it. I'll be back down in a few minutes." He stayed with one foot up and one foot on the stair below. "Make yourself comfortable, maybe find the remote and watch TV."

"I'll be fine. Would it be okay if I sat on the deck? It's so nice out."

"Of course. I'll hurry."

Jasper stood in the shower leaning against the wall under the shower, helpless to his feelings for Dobson. If only he could trust her not to treat him like an object, he might be able to live a good life being himself. But even his parents didn't let him do that, how could he expect that from her?

He quickly scrubbed off remnants of the lake and beach, toweled off, and dressed in his shorts and a dark shirt that could withstand ketchup or mustard spilling on it. He pulled on his tennis shoes and raced downstairs.

"I'm ready," he told her, and grabbed the food he was bringing to his brother's house and placed it in a bag. "We're walking. Do you mind?"

She beamed. "Not at all." She opened her hands. "What can I carry?"

"I've got it covered." He strode outside with her by his side and they headed up the beach again. Thoughts swirled in his mind but none of them were worth saying out loud. Dobson's pace was fast and she didn't miss anything, commenting on the sounds of seagulls flying nearby and the slap, slap, slapping of waves.

"You're close to your family, aren't you?" she asked.

"I'm close to my brothers. I love my parents but they can be a bit much."

"How?"

"They are needy. I'm happy to help them around the house or the yard or whatever. But they rely on me to be the entertainment committee, always keeping the peace, and being the funny guy who keeps everyone laughing. They don't realize I'm not a gangly teenager any more. Probably typical parents. I'm not complaining. My job gives me anxiety but I'm proud of what I do. I'm content working for the ambulance service, helping out Gray, and enjoying lake life." Here he went again, revealing private things to her.

"I don't know what's typical. My mother has ideas about what she'd like for me but overall she wants me to live my life, not her idea of it," Dobson said. "I think that's healthy."

"That would be nice." Jasper shifted the bag of dinner foods to his other arm. "I just need to work out a few things that drag me down. My parents are great."

"I know. I've met them, remember?"

Jasper chuckled. "Oh yeah. Your mom was nice, too. You two seem close."

"We are. Ever since my dad was killed, she and I have been close. We take care of each other. I cherish her." Her voice dropped.

He could see her struggling with tears. "It's hard to lose a loved one."

"So very hard. And it keeps on hurting." Dobson looked away, sniffing. "I'm sorry for getting gloomy about something that happened when I was a child."

"Don't be. It takes as long as it takes." He picked up a smooth, flat rock and skipped it across the water.

"That was a good toss." Her heart lifted at the carefree motion.

"What did your dad do for a living?" Jasper asked.

"He was an FBI agent. He was killed in the line of duty. His death was one reason I went into police work. You know, righting wrongs."

The sparkle returning to Dobson's eyes confirmed that she had needed to share her loss with him. He took hold of one of her hands and squeezed. "Your dad would be very proud of what you're doing."

"Thank you. I appreciate your kindness, Jasper. You've been so understanding. I'm not used to that. People all around me expect me to be over my dad's death."

"They're probably uncomfortable with you being sad, but that's their problem." He switched hands again with the food so he could open the door to Rhys's house for her. "We're here," he called.

"Hi Jasper, Dobson," Gray said. "I'm glad you could make it."

"Yeah," Rachel agreed. "You're just in time for dinner. We were just talking about your culinary skills, Jasper."

"So, what's for dinner?" Rhys tossed a pillow at him, but Jasper ducked.

"I brought burgers to grill and my special Asian coleslaw." Jasper sensed Dobson was still warming to the room. He put the bags of food on the counter and gave her a wink. "What did you bring, Rhys?"

"I'm providing condiments," he said, leaning back in his chair and stretching his arms.

"I brought desert," spoke up Cherish. "It's my special made-from-scratch red velvet cupcakes."

"Oo, let's have desert first," Dobson chimed in.

Rhys sat up straight and pointed to Dobson. "You are right, let's do that."

Jasper was glad to see her relax and join in. It took a weight off his shoulders. "I'll start grilling these burgers so we can eat soon."

"Good. I'll set the table. Anything else you need help with just let me know. I'm starving," said Rhys, rising and walking to the kitchen.

Dobson followed him out to the deck and helped him place the burgers on the gas grill. "I appreciate your help but you can stay with the group inside if you'd like."

"I'm fine here with you." Her voice sounded confident and comfortable.

"I am fine with you here." Everything inside him wanted to grab her close, touch her skin, feel her soft lips on his. She distracted his mind, made it challenging to go through the motions of the mundane. "How do you do that?"

"Do what?" Something flicked in her eyes. "I'm just standing here talking with you. Do you want me to shut up?"

"I meant, how do you distract me so much and at the same time make everything extraordinary?"

"Oh." Dobson stared at him. "You feel like that?"

"Yes?" He'd taken the risk and now was it just awkward for her? "I mean, yes, I do." He couldn't breathe, waiting for her response.

"I think we should talk about this. But not right now," she said, looking back at the house. "Too many windows in Rhys's kitchen."

That didn't go exactly as he planned. He wanted to kiss her. "Sure, sure. We need fewer prying eyes and ears. I get it." He turned away from her and checked the burgers. "I should attend to these anyway."

Laughter came from inside the house mixed with loud talking.

"Sounds like they're having a good time. I'll go check out what's going on." She gave him a smile and walked inside.

She went inside without responding to him. Jasper refrained from watching her. He'd made it clear he was attracted to her and she'd ignored it.

CHAPTER 17

*D*obson carried her head high as she walked inside Rhys's house, ready to face his family as friends. It sent shivers through her to think of being so unguarded. But she was up to trying.

"Dobson, come and sit down. The Tigers' game is starting." Cherish patted the spot on the couch next to her. "We're all serious baseball fans, specifically, Tigers fans."

Dobson eased into the couch. Managing her nerves took effort, but willingness boosted her confidence. "I am a fan of baseball."

"Yes, I knew you would be," cheered Rhys.

"Specifically, I'm a Cubs fan."

"Ohhh…" they all groaned.

She laughed heartily, relaxing her shoulders. "Sorry to disappoint. I'm from Chicago, you know. How are the Tigers doing this season?"

"Well, they're doing poorly," Gray said. "They're playing about five-hundred ball."

"The Cubs have a four-game winning streak going on." Cherish crossed her fingers. "We have high hopes for that to continue."

"Are we talking baseball?" Jasper asked, walking in carrying the grilled burgers. "I recognize those stats. The Tigers are hitting the ball better." He placed the plate of burgers and bowl of coleslaw on the table. "Come get food."

"Sounds like they're playing well. So far. What place are they in their division?" Dobson asked, eyeing the burgers and noticing her stomach growl.

Jasper handed a plate to Dobson. "I hope you like buffet-style. The Tigers are in third place, eight games out of first. How are the Cubs doing?"

She finished chewing a grilled potato slice. "They're struggling. Not hitting very well. Their defense is really good but they're not giving the pitchers much help. They're in fourth place."

She sat down in the living room and balanced her plate on her knees. A smile in her heart gave her a warm feeling that bordered on belonging.

It got quiet around the room for a moment but it felt natural to her.

"You've watched some baseball," Rhys commented. "You know your stuff."

"Like I said, I'm a baseball fan. I like to watch the Cubs, especially when they're winning."

"Oh, I'm so sorry. Cubs hardly ever win," teased Rhys. "You do sound like an ardent fan."

"I know my way around a baseball field. I played ball in high school."

"Good grief!" Jasper exclaimed. "You're full of surprises. What position?"

"Short stop. My team made it to finals my senior year. But one of the most thrilling moments in my life was walking into Wrigley Field to watch the Cubs play. My dad scored some tickets on the sidelines between home and first base. I was only eight years old and it was just me and my dad sitting in the stands. We got to see a lot of action." Realization set in that she'd been mesmerized by her own memories and kept the center of attention for some time. She pulled in and shrunk back down. "I better stop talking so much so we can watch the game."

"No, no. worries," Rachel said. "I'm glad you like baseball, you'll fit right in." She bit into her burger and talked with her mouth full. "Jasper, this is delicious."

"Thanks. It's pretty simple to grill stuff."

Dobson's heart skipped at his smile. It was a little lopsided, but just enough to catch her attention. She sat processing the interaction between everyone. They all were skilled at communication and conversation slid easily between each one. No one was ignored. She almost belonged.

She'd just finished eating when Gray took her plate to the counter, then sat down in a chair near her. Her muscles tightened, preparing for whatever might ensue, but she consciously relaxed to hold onto the sense that she was in a safe place.

"We should talk," he said.

"Okay. What do you want to talk about?" She crossed her legs and lifted her chin.

"Chicago, of course. I lived there for a few years and I understand you're fresh from living there. Did you love it there?"

She couldn't suppress the memories. "I didn't know anything different until about three weeks ago when I moved to Dunes Bay. Loved it? I loved lots of things about Chicago," she hedged. "Did you love it? You were probably right in the thick of things, being a reporter."

"I like the frenetic vibe of the place. Everyone is very busy trying to get somewhere. It's invigorating. Gathering news was death defying. But Chicago and its politics got inside my blood." He shook his head and gazed at her with depth in his eyes.

Oh, he's another clear-eyed Steele brother. She liked his directness and that presence Steele men had. His thirst for life was almost as vivid as Jasper's. "Where else can you get a deep-dish pizza Chicago-style that is yummy?"

"Nowhere but Lou Malnati's. Where else can you live in a high-rise looking over the city and one of the Great Lakes? I miss it."

"Why did you leave? Chicago has everything you could want. And in multiples." She chuckled.

"You could write a travel piece." Gray's eyes clouded. "It even has some bad cops. I had to leave town in order to avoid being killed and to ensure my family wasn't in jeopardy because of me. Unfortunately, those cops were tenacious. They followed me here."

Her hand went to her mouth. "Oh my god, you're kidding." But by the look on his face, she knew he wasn't.

"Nope. Not kidding," Rhys interjected. "I know because Jasper and I helped rescue Cherish from the bad cops."

"That's right, brothers. You make a good team," added Gray. "But all of that is in the past and everything is fine now."

"Fine for you. Now Dobson is the one of us getting death threats." Jasper stood behind her and rested his hands on her shoulders.

His touch soothed her, grounded her, and she knew he was beginning to understand her, and wished for an opportunity to talk with him privately.

"I'm on board," Gray said, talking over food in his mouth.

"Of course I'm your man." Rhys wiped his face with a napkin, his eyes never leaving the television. "Don't swing at those low balls," he yelled. "Did you see that?"

"Yes I did," said Rachel. "Two strikes on this guy and he swings at a low ball."

"Anyway, I'm happy in Dunes Bay," Gray said. "Cherish showed me there was so much good in life here that I stayed." He grabbed Cherish and hugged her.

"You two seem very happy." Dobson couldn't envy them their love. It was a beautiful thing that made the world a better place.

"Okay you two. If you're going to do that get a room," Rhys teased. "You're missing the ballgame."

"Brother, I'm not missing anything," said Gray, and kissed Cherish.

"All this hugging and kissing going on makes me want to get some fresh air. Dobson, would you like to go to the top of the lighthouse with me?"

Dobson stood and walked toward the door. "I don't know if I can climb all those stairs as fast as you can, but I'm eager to try," she joked.

Gray stood. "Before you leave, I wanted to tell you that I recently wrote a piece for the Chicago newspaper about a successful new treatment for lung cancer. I can text you the link to the article if you'd like. Your mother mentioned her illness when we were all at Jasper's house."

"I didn't know that. Please, send me the link." She lowered her gaze. "My mom believes her impending death is inevitable. I have to accept that may be true, but I'm interested in fighting the cancer."

OUTSIDE, Dobson stared up toward the top of Rhys's lighthouse in awe.

"Are you ready to go up top?" Jasper stood beside her, shading his eyes. "It's awesome up there. Let's go."

"How many steps are there?"

"I don't know, but the top of the tower at the lantern room is a one-hundred-thirty-two-foot high climb." Jasper led her through the hallway at the back of Rhys's house and opened the door to the stairs. "This is going to change your life."

Dobson laughed. "I doubt that. I'm game. I'll follow you."

The stairs wound around the spiral staircase. The air inside the tower chilled her skin. "Are you doing all right?" she asked Jasper.

"Hah, I could climb this in my sleep. I hope you're not afraid of heights."

"I guess we'll find out." Her breaths were coming harder. "Are we almost there?"

"Yup. Just a little farther." Jasper picked up his pace as they rounded another circle. "Good thing you're an athlete." He looked over his shoulder at her and gave her a thumbs up.

"Former athlete. But I'm, uh, fine." She tried to catch her breath.

They reached the last step and Jasper opened the door.

Dobson gasped. "I don't know what to say. It's a beautiful view," she said, walking around the deck encircling the glass lantern room.

"I understand. The experience of being up here is unlike anything else. My first time I never wanted to leave." Jasper said, looking out over the lake.

Dobson looked up at the darkening sky and pointed. "A few stars are out. This is amazing. It's breezier up here," she said. The wind tossed her hair in her face and she moved it behind her ears, laughing. "I'm mesmerized."

"I know I am." His deep voice was seductive.

She turned to face him and found him staring at her. A shiver drifted through her.

"Are you cold?"

She peered into his eyes. "No."

Everything around fell away as he pulled her close. He pressed a gentle kiss to her cheek, her forehead, behind her ear. She closed her eyes and lifted her lips to his. He brushed hers with his lips, then leaned against her. The firmness of his body stopped her breath in her chest and she closed her eyes, anticipating.

His lips pressed against hers and swept her away. When he pulled back, she looked up into an expression of deep emotion on his face.

"Is this a dream?" she asked. "If it is, I don't want to wake up." She ran her fingers over his lips. Their softness and warmth tantalized her.

"It's real." He turned her to face out toward the lake. "Listen."

She stilled and heard the crash of waves falling upon themselves. The rhythmic sound matched the dark waves below and invigorated her heart. "It's all so beautiful," she breathed. "Rhys is lucky."

"He is. But as beautiful as all this is, you're the one who is beautiful, and I'm the one who is lucky."

"I think I'm getting dizzy, all these sweet words," she said. "Thank you for an amazing day. And this," she stretched her arms wide, "is more than I could ever hope to experience."

"I wanted to share this with you. I knew you'd appreciate the uncanny beauty." He caressed her cheek. "We probably should rejoin the party." His wistful look stirred her emotions.

"I suppose we should. Not before I tell you that earlier when you tried to talk to me about personal stuff, I didn't mean to sound curt or cut you off. I simply wanted privacy." She walked close to the railing and leaned on one foot. "I'm not ready to make a lifelong commitment. But I hope we can get past our rather bumpy beginning and be friends, more than friends. Your family is special, and you are something else. Is it time we state the obvious, that we want a relationship with each other, or is it too soon? I don't want to jinx it."

"I can't tell you when you're ready. But, are you superstitious? Wish on one of those stars up there for what you want and trust your instincts. Feel your feelings. Don't become your emotions. They can be fear-based and warn you away based on past experiences. Your gut will lead you in the right direction."

"I'm not superstitious, but what you're saying is making me believe in magic," she said, gazing up at the sky. "You were right about one thing. Up here things look different. My perspective has been small and fearful. I don't want to do that anymore. I want to open to new possibilities and even magic." Dobson laughed at herself. "I sound so silly."

"I don't think so. What better way to find your true self than to open to unexpected opportunities." Jasper sighed as though letting go of a heavy weight.

Back in the house, Dobson said her thank yous and good byes along with Jasper, then they began walking back to his place. The mood was subdued, thoughtful. She liked that they chatted on and off, but felt comfortable with nothing but the sounds around them. There were no blank moments when they weren't talking, just rich presence that filled her with bliss.

When they arrived back at Jasper's place he took her hand and stood on the edge of the water with her. "Stay with me a minute?" he asked. "Look at that view. I keep saying that. I'm impressed with it. I know there are beautiful views all over the world, but this one is right in front of us."

"I'm impressed too. Look at how the moonlight glitters on the dark lake, almost making a path to itself." She didn't want to break the moment, but parts of her felt so cheesy she could hardly stand it. She had to sit on her impulse to laugh out loud.

"That's poetic," he said. "I know you feel awkward about letting yourself express creatively, but you don't have to with me. Besides, I'm the one who suggested you wish on a star."

"I like it. Can we just stand here quietly for a little longer? It's so perfect here."

He pulled her hand up to his lips and kissed it reverently. Their gazes collided and he lifted her chin. "This is a perfect moment. Thank you for sharing it with me." He kissed her passionately and she felt like she could lift off.

CHAPTER 18

Jasper grabbed Dobson's hand and together they walked inside. He bent closer and held his breath, hoping she'd allow him to kiss her, just one more time. She closed her eyes and lifted her lips to meet his. Her lips were soft, responsive, and he pressed harder. Her hands on either side of his head held him. His heart hammered in his chest and he wanted more of her.

Dobson opened her eyes and looked starry-eyed. "That was nice," she said.

"I agree." He ran his thumb over her warm lips. "I'm either going to explode or drop to the floor dead tired. How are you feeling?"

Laughter bubbled out of her. "I think you nailed it. It's been a busy, exhilarating day. I think I'll hit the sack."

His smile melted her. "Yeah, I'm not sure how much energy I have left." He put a kiss to her cheek and brushed his hand over her hair. "Make yourself at home. I hope you sleep well tonight."

"You too." She took the stairs up to the room he'd given her while he turned off the downstairs lights and locked the doors.

Upstairs in his bedroom, Jasper stripped and jumped in bed. He lay in the dark, listening to small sounds in the room on the other side of his wall. When he'd heard the water running in the shower his thoughts went to imagining Dobson naked and sweet-smelling, like fresh rain. But he squashed those thoughts and tried to focus on his breathing.

They had made a good choice. It was better this way, with no sex and sleeping peacefully.

Who was he kidding? He tossed and turned, sat up, then lay back down. The covers were too scratchy. He threw them off, and stared up at the ceiling. Focusing on the sounds of the beach coming from outside, relaxation heavied his eyelids. His mind wouldn't stop. Thoughts of the day kept circling inside his head, followed by memories of the evening with Dobson. Frustration churned. He had to get to sleep.

A floor joist squeaked and he froze. Then he heard the bedroom door open quietly. He sat up in bed, not sure if he should grab one of his bats in case it was an intruder or open his arms.

"I would like to lie with you."

He instantly relaxed, knowing it was Dobson standing in the darkness. He could make out shiny sparkles and a hint of lace. "Come on in," he said, opening the covers for her to slide in beside him. She snuggled close and he wrapped his arm around her shoulders. "Are you cold?" he asked.

"No." She sucked at his lower lip, then kissed under his chin.

"Are you sure? I don't have any agenda for tonight."

"It feels right. I couldn't stop thinking about you," Dobson whispered. "If you don't want to have sex, that's all right. I'll understand."

Jasper rolled on top of her and kissed her lips, hard.

She giggled. "I guess you couldn't sleep either."

She drew her pajamas over her head and pulled him down to lie on top of her, skin to skin.

Her skin heated beneath him and his body grew excited. "You feel so good," Jasper groaned.

"Wait, I think I hear my phone ringing." Her ears perked to the sound.

"Can't you ignore it?" he asked, snuggling against her neck.

"I can't. That's the ring for my mom. She wouldn't call me at this hour unless something is wrong." She scrambled to her feet and ran to the other bedroom.

Jasper's muscles twitched at the thought that something bad was happening. He got up and grabbed his robe from a hook in the closet and went to her. He wrapped the robe around her as he waited. Her eyes were wide and she chewed on her thumbnail.

"Mom, the only thing that matters is if you're all right. Did he hurt you? Okay, that's good. I'm sure it was upsetting. I'll be right home."

Selfishly, Jasper's heart sunk. It seemed like every time he and Dobson came close to physical intimacy, something interrupted.

"A man knocked on Mom's door and told her it was urgent he speak to her. A matter of life and death." An expression of a mixture of anger and tears on her face sent chills through him. She ran her fingers through her hair, looking stunned.

"Oh my god! I should have realized your mother could be in the mob's crosshairs." He slammed his fist against the wall.

"I should have known better than to leave her alone all day and night. Teddy's people are probably watching my apartment. Either one of them or Wynne dropped by. Take a number. Who wants to blow up my life next?" She quickly started pulling clothes from her suitcase.

He put his hands on her shoulders. "She'll be okay until we get back to your condo. It will take me one second to dress and you're almost dressed already."

She let out a heavy sigh. "You don't need to go with me. I don't want you in trouble either. Besides, you have to go to work today."

"Of course I'm coming with. Not because you need me, but because I can't not go. You let me worry about my work." He turned her around to face him. "If you tell me to stay away, I'll do what you ask."

Dobson leaned her head on his chest and said nothing. He put his arms around her and held her.

"I don't know how to accept your help. I've been on my own for so long, taking care of things, taking care of Mom."

"It doesn't have to mean you're weak. It just means we're in this together, and that's a good thing." Jasper tweaked a lock of her hair. It was soft and flawless, even though it stood out from her head like a crown of ivy.

"Okay, you go get ready. I would like you to go. But hurry!"

As soon as Jasper sprinted to his room she finished dressing, stuffing her revolver into the holster at her back. "I'm ready," she called out.

"Me too," Jasper called through her door. "I'm going to the car."

She heard him run down the stairs and followed him to the front door. He was holding a bat. She eyed him with a smirk.

"I'm a bat guy, not a gun person."

"I get it. I have the gun, so we're covered." Her solemn face made him hesitate.

"You sure you don't want to call for back up? Just to be safe." He fidgeted with his key, feeling a storm of emotions.

"No. I've been here on the force for only two and a half weeks. I'm not going to show weakness already," she said. "Besides, there should be cops guarding our home."

"It's up to you," Jasper said.

"Follow me," she said.

He climbed into his truck and sped away toward town. Dobson's face worried him. It was a picture of desperation and strain, but he hadn't pressed her to share her thoughts or work out a plan. His heart went out to her, wanting to assure her everything would be okay. But he realized, from her perspective, nothing had been okay since her father's murder.

He drove into the parking area in front of Dobson's condo. Dobson climbed out her car before he put the truck in park. She dashed inside without him, but he was close behind.

Dobson stood quietly at the door, her gun drawn, and listened. She motioned to him to stand on the opposite side. He'd never had a gun, but the bat in his hands gave him confidence.

She nodded at the officer posted at the front and silently crept by him.

At the front door, Dobson slowly turned the doorknob. It was locked, so she carefully unlocked it and cracked open the door. They peered in. Her mother was perched on the edge of the couch.

Dobson flew to her, and Jasper ran in behind her, alert to any strangers inside. He checked the other rooms, his bat held high, but saw no one.

"The other rooms are clear," he said in the hallway.

He walked in to the living room to find Dobson and Cecilia hugging.

"I didn't know what to do other than call you, sweetheart," her mother said into Dobson's shoulder. "I'm sorry if I woke you. I'm glad to see you brought backup. Thank you for coming, Jasper."

"Of course. What did the men look like?"

"Sit down, Mom. I'll sit beside you." Dobson eased her mother onto the couch.

"There were two of them. One was short and stocky, had dark hair, a mustache, and shiny shoes. The other one had dark hair too, but he was taller than the other one and didn't say anything. He stood beside the shorter guy and glared at me with dark eyes. He had a long, straight nose and a scar on his chin," Cecilia said. Her knuckles were white as she clutched the arm of the couch. Jasper went to the kitchen and got her a glass of water.

"Here, drink this," he said. "I know the experience was terrifying but you're okay now. I want to take your pulse."

"He's right, Mom. You can relax." Dobson rubbed her mom's arm. "You're freezing." She wrapped an afghan around her mother's shoulders.

"I'm fine, I'm fine. Stop making over me. I need to tell you what the man said." Tears trickled down her cheeks. "I'm not the one in danger. It's you, Dobson. He told me to warn you that if you don't stop snooping in the organization's business there will be problems you can't imagine." Cecilia rested her head against the back of the couch.

Jasper took Dobson's hand and led her to kitchen. "We'll be just a minute," he told Cecilia.

"What do you think? Was the visitor someone you know?"

She rung her hands and stared out the kitchen window. "She's not far from going into shock. I think she'll be okay but she is not fine. Or safe," she said. She turned to him. "I think it was Teddy's nephew, Franco Ricci. I suspect the other one is Soren Lucia. Geez, this is my fault. I was selfish to think I could get away for a good time even just one day." She slid down to the floor and held her head in her hands.

Jasper dropped down beside her. "You didn't do anything wrong."

"Hmph."

"No, I'm serious. It will be morning soon. The two of you will eat breakfast, and I'll make sure protection services are planning to spend the day and night. You'll go to work. You'll be worried, but not guilty of anything that caused the men to threaten your mom."

"It's hard to drop old patterns. I'm so used to taking responsibility for every hint of a mistake. But it's a choice, I know." Dobson starred at him. "You're something else, for sure."

He smiled at her. "You're a warrior."

"Get out." Dobson began rising and Jasper helped her up.

"You are. As for your mother, her pulse is high. I don't think she's in shock, but I would like to give her a little sedative if she'll let me. Just to help her sleep for a while. It would be good for her to sleep."

"That sounds good. Thank you."

"See, I can be helpful." He laughed. "I can stay, but you probably would like me to get out of here so you can do what you need to do next."

"I do need to make some phone calls and see if I can go into the office for that."

Her mind was working, he could tell, attacking the problem full strength. "You better get some sleep too," he suggested. "Our night was cut short."

"About that, I don't know what to say. I was eager for intimacy, but we keep getting interrupted. Maybe our timing is off."

His heart dropped. "Maybe. I'd like to keep trying. One of these times we'll get what we want."

"I'd like to believe that."

"I'll believe for the both of us for now. How about that?"

She looped her arms over his neck and kissed him once.

CHAPTER 19

Dobson cracked open her mother's bedroom door to the sound of soft snoring. Relieved, she closed it again and headed to her own room. It was five o'clock in the morning, she noted, and lay down to try to get a little bit more shut eye.

She stared up at the ceiling in the early morning light with gratitude for Jasper's help filling her heart. This wasn't the first time she'd felt it. He kept on being there when she needed him and gave her space when that was all she wanted.

A little voice inside spoke up. It's only been five days. She rolled over, annoyance agitating her nerves. She knew the belief that the good stuff he offered wouldn't last was warning her to keep her safe. But she couldn't help but trust her gut, which told her he was a good man. "Go away!" she yelled into her pillow. The walls of protection were beginning to smother her.

She threw off the covers and walked to her kitchen for breakfast. Impatience streamed through her for arranging for protection for her mother. As soon as it was time for Hector's shift to come on duty she would call and set things in motion. She didn't trust anyone but Hector.

She sipped coffee and drummed her fingers on the counter top, her brain reckoning with her guilt. Painful and incessant, the guilt hit her in her chest, over and over. She should never have gotten involved with Wynne. Hell, she could have just let the dirty cops continue with their crimes and she wouldn't be hiding her in Dunes Bay. And yesterday, she should never have taken the day for pleasure.

Regret twisted her stomach like a tourniquet. Instead of running from the sick feeling in her stomach, she remained with it. Riding it out was unthinkable, but it was necessary if she wanted freedom from the pain. Her insides scrambled to get away from the hard truth that she made choices and had to deal with the consequences.

A turmoil of emotions stormed inside her, pushing her to get up and pace the floor. She rubbed her forehead, struggling to contain them all. Tears brimmed her eyes and streamed down her face.

If she could sort through all the bad things, maybe she could deflate their power over her. Maybe Jasper was right, that negative emotions can be managed by feeling them until there was no negativity.

She had so many questions. How could she have known that Wynne was married? It was he who betrayed her and not the other way around. He'd lied and if she were at fault for something it was for being naïve.

It dawned on her that she was putting together things that weren't connected. She'd simply followed her values of justice and ethics by reporting the dirty cops. They were held accountable, and that was a good thing for a police department. She wasn't responsible for anyone's death, not even Bryan Murdoch's suicide.

That was what echoed through her and sent her to the floor in a pile. There were things she couldn't control. She had to be able to contain that and accept that others were responsible for their own lives, good or bad.

Dobson wrapped her arms around her middle and rocked on the floor. The implication hurt her heart. Of course, it was true. It made sense. But it also meant she couldn't stop her mother from dying. She couldn't have done anything to prevent her father's murder. And she might soon be all alone in the world, surrounded by people but none who she belonged to, could count on, or who would cherish her for being herself.

Grief, powerful, blood curdling grief shook her, and she trembled uncontrollably. But reason argued with it.

She had her mother, and if she could get her involved with a study, she might be able to save her. It was up to her to keep her alive.

She could make Wynne see that he was better off without her and that she wasn't to blame for the other officer's suicide.

She could work harder to connect Teddy to Devin's murder and keep everyone around her safer.

A tiny little flame of a voice spoke up. It's not your job to take care of everyone in the manner you see fit. You have to respect self-determination and individual choice.

Her feelings shifted, and relief drifted over her, warming her like a fire. Understanding bloomed of her place in the world and her own self-determination. She stood to her feet, a sense of strength and courage pervading. It was an understanding that felt a little shaky. She suspected it would take some doing to let go of the false beliefs she'd been living from, but change is always a challenge. Longing to be herself would guide her to live by her values.

A list of priorities popped up in her mind:

•Check in with Hector

•Shower and go into the office

•Call Jasper

•Figure out possible suspects for the murder of Devin Raye

The important thing was she had a plan. The rest would come to her.

The clock on her bedside table told her it was finally eight o'clock and that Hector would be at the department. She made her phone call about ensuring her mother stayed safe, and Hector assured her he would handle it immediately after hanging up. She'd given him details and he agreed it needed to be done ASAP.

"Thanks, Hector. I owe you one."

"Listen, you take care of yourself, you hear?" he demanded

"Of course."

The doorbell rang and she ran to the door before the bell could awaken her mother. "Hello, can I help you?" she asked through the door, her hand on her gun.

"Are you Dobson Ramirez?"

She cracked the door open with her foot braced against it and saw a young man in jeans and a bright colored T-shirt holding an armful of flowers.

"Yes."

He shoved the bouquet in her face. "These are for you. Have a great day," he added, smiling widely.

"Wait, who are these from?" she called after him.

"The card is attached."

Dobson hurried inside and closed the door. She took pains to be quiet and put the flowers on the kitchen counter, where she dug into the bouquet of roses and baby's-breath.

"Did Jasper send you flowers, dear?" Her mother walked into the kitchen, still in her robe and slippers.

"I don't know who gave them to me. I'm searching for a card." Triumphant, she held up the card. "I found it."

She tore open the card and read to herself. "Dobson, I miss you and what we had. Please meet me for coffee at a little place I found, Darcy's Dinner, at noon. We have unfinished business."

Her mouth dry, Dobson swallowed hard. But she wanted to see him to tell him once and for all to leave her alone.

"The flowers are not from Jasper, Mom. They're from someone I knew in Chicago." She threw the flowers in the trash and stood erect. "They don't mean anything to me. I have to go to the office. I'm running a little late."

"Okay," said her mom, sitting in a kitchen chair. "Don't worry about me."

"Well, I do. And for good reason. So, I've arranged for police offi-cers to stand outside the condo and keep watch over you. You don't have to engage with them or give them coffee. They are doing a job I want them to focus hard on."

"What about you? Who is going to watch over you?" Cecilia said, her eyes sharp.

"I'm a cop. I can take care of myself." Dobson remembered she was wearing shorts and a tank top and walked toward the bedroom.

"So can I." Her mother's voice was stern.

"Mom," she said softly, walking back into the kitchen. "Of course you can. But not if someone has a gun or throws you down on the floor. These people are brutal. They'll do anything to get to me." Reality registered with her mother at the same moment as it did with Dobson. Her mother could be in serious trouble because of her.

She started to speak, but her mother interrupted her.

"I like your spunk, daughter. But put that to use in your own life and let me live mine."

Speechless, Dobson stood beside her with her mouth open.

"I know your intentions are good and I appreciate your concern. But the last thing I want in my life is to make you small just to take care of me."

"Mom, don't say that. You are everything to me. You've sacrificed so much. I want to help you."

"Let's not argue, dear. Just listen to what I'm saying and try not to worry so much," Cecilia said.

"I hear you. No promises." Dobson didn't have to like what her mother said, and she didn't.

She dressed for work keeping an eye out for the expected officers. When they didn't arrive, she gave her mother strict instructions. Don't open the door to anyone. Use the peek hole to identify anyone who comes to the door. Hopefully it will be the officers assigned to you. If it's not, call me immediately. I've got to go."

"No te preocupes por mi," her mom said again.

"But I do worry about you."

"Te amo, Mija."

"I love you too. Te quiero, Mamá.

At the department, Dobson stopped to speak with Hector at the front desk.

"Good morning," he said. "I'm sorry to hear you had an uninvited guest bother your mom. I've put one officer at the front entrance to your condo and another at the back. Did you see them before you left home?"

"No. I wanted to wait for them but it was getting late. I needed to get to work to check on some things, then I'm going back out again. Could you contact them to make sure they've arrived?"

"Sure. I'll let you know," he said and picked up the mic to his radio.

Dobson hurried in to her office and sat down in front of her computer. First, she called Jasper.

"Hi there." His jovial voice made her smile.

"Hi. I'm at work but I wanted to thank you for your input last night with my mom. It really helped my brain sort out what I needed to do."

"I've been telling you, we make a good team. How's your mom today?"

"Spunky. Yes, spunky is the word I would use. I told her I ordered protection service for her and she told me to mind my own business."

"No, she told you that?" Jasper laughed. "I guess she's feeling better. Good."

"No, not good. I need her to comply. I'm just looking out for her."

"I know. But what is her message?"

"She made it quite clear she doesn't want me to worry about her."

"I get that. But what is her message? What is she not saying?" Jasper asked.

"Maybe she's tired of having no say about her life. Sort of like the cancer and me are taking over."

"Ask her?" he suggested.

"Right. Well, I've got to go. Have a good day, Jasper."

He sighed. "I love it when you say my name. It feels personal."

She paused.

"Are you there?" he asked

"I am. I was thinking about what you said. It sounds nice. I'm glad you told me."

She hung up and collected her thoughts. Jasper was always surprising her with unexpected thoughts. Life spilled out of him, and she was enjoying being close.

Shaking her head to center her thoughts, she opened a file of possible suspects in the Devin Raye case and ran through the list to match pictures to the description of the men her mother described. Frustrated it was taking so long, she stopped herself from scrolling through the pictures too fast.

She was interrupted in her search when her phone rang. It was Hector on the line.

"I just talked to the officers. They're standing guard as we speak. They saw you driving down the street. Apparently they arrived just after you left.'

Relief fluttered in her stomach. "Thank you for checking, Hector. You're the best."

"I know," he teased and hung up.

She returned her focus to the faces in her file, hoping she would find the man who threatened her mom.

Then, just like that, his picture stood out on the page. She blinked, blinked, and bit on her lower lip.

It had to be him. The man in the picture had a scar on his chin, dark hair, and deep brown eyes. His name was Soren Lucia.

"Gotcha."

Dobson did a quick search on the suspect and learned he'd had several arrests for robbery and assault. Married once, divorced. Known associates included people who also had records. Her eyes froze in place suddenly on a name she knew well—Teddy Esposito.

She stood up abruptly and started pacing. What did this mean? Obviously, she needed to check out the connection between Soren and Teddy. Could it be that Soren was one of Teddy's muscle men?

She looked deeper and deeper. Soren was a real estate developer who owned several commercial properties. He'd also been cited for leaving his apartment complex tenants without heat last winter and he'd had complaints about pests in the buildings and water in the basements.

Could he be committing his crimes under the radar, while expanding his relationship with the Espositos?

Dobson printed the pages related to Soren and put them in her bag. She sat back at her desk and called Zachary on his cell phone.

"Hi Dobson," he answered. "What's up?"

"Do you know a guy named Soren Lucia? I think he's the man with Marco Esposito who threatened my mother."

"Dirt bag," Zachary muttered. "I'm sorry that happened. You knew the Espositos would come after you, but that's pretty low. Yes, I know him. He's graduated from petty crimes to assault with a deadly weapon and much, much more. He's been inducted into the Espositos for managing the drug side of their business and as an enforcer. A real peach."

"Sounds like it. I might be able to connect him with Teddy for killing Devin Raye. It's time for another arrest, I'm thinking."

Zachary chuckled. "Yes, let's turn up the heat."

"Thanks for this info. I'll keep you posted. Probably at the meeting Friday."

"Great. See you soon."

Dobson grabbed her bag along with her purse and headed to a coffee break she didn't have time for, but it was time to confront Wynne.

* * *

THE CALL they'd taken was simple, a mistaken heart attack that just required a prescription strength antacid. But Jasper and Tavis had transported the guy to the ER for care, in case something else more dire was the problem. The doctor would take a look at him and probably release him. Now on their way back to house, Jasper listened to Tavis talk about his new lawnmower, and got the picture. "So you're in love with your mower. Have you mowed your lawn with it yet?"

"Not yet. But you're missing the point. It's going to make mowing so much easier, so I'll cut the grass more often. Happy neighbors and happy girlfriend." He winked.

"Awesome." Jasper turned away and rolled his eyes. Tavis's lawn was a postage stamp. "Whatever trips your trigger."

He shouldn't be so disdainful of Tavis's mower obsession. He had his own obsession, and it was Dobson. She was the kind of person who fascinated him, not for her perfection but because she was raw. She had suffered trauma from violence, threats to her life, loss, bullying, yet she bravely stuck to her mission: right wrongs and help people. He respected that. He could overlook her simmering temperament, especially because along with the anger it gave her spark.

"You got quiet," Tavis said, interrupting his thoughts of Dobson.

"I'm just daydreaming."

"Before we take this rig back to the house, let's think about lunch," Tavis said.

"Sure." Jasper stared out the window and watched the city go by. He'd never dreamed of moving away from his home town. It had always been home. As long as his brothers lived here and he had a job, he'd stay. Still, he wanted to be open to new opportunities, ones that fed his soul and didn't tear him up inside. He could do without the deaths he faced every day and tried so hard to prevent. The mixture of emotions growled in his gut.

"Is lunch anywhere in our near future." Tavis rubbed his belly.

"Yeah, things are slow, knock on wood."

Tavis rapped his fist on Jasper's head.

"Get off of me," Jasper fumed. "Very funny. You'd be better off knocking on your blockhead."

"At any rate, Bertie's is just up ahead. I love those subs."

"Let's do it." Jasper liked being on call with Tavis, so Jasper put aside his frustration with being teased. Tavis was laid back and fun-loving, but when a call came in he jumped into action. His bedside manner was professional, and he always did a good job of soothing patients' fears.

A few blocks up, Tavis turned the ambulance into the restaurant and stopped at the drive-up window to order. "I know what you want. Portabella mushroom with extra cheese and tomatoes," he said.

"It's my regular." Jasper's mouth started to water already. "And you'll have the Bert's Italian sub with everything. I know you well, my friend."

The food was ready quickly and they drove under a tree in the parking lot of a small park. Jasper watched Tavis throw back his sandwich. Of course he did. Time was precious. Any moment a call might come in.

Tavis moaned. Through an oversized bite in his mouth, he spoke. "This is what I'm talking about. This sandwich is a masterpiece."

The radio came alive. "2216 we got a vehicle and a motorcycle accident at the intersection of 25th and Maple. One person is on the ground, face down. One person may have been shot. What is your ETA?"

"We're eight minutes out," Jasper responded.

He turned on the siren and Tavis kicked down the accelerator. Lunch time was not the best time to weave through traffic and red lights, but Tavis was a master with the horn.

He pulled up to the intersection and parked out of the way of traffic as best he could. A police officer hurried up.

"Hey, Jordan. What's going on here?" Tavis asked.

"We've got one biker down on the pavement after a gunshot wound to his leg. In the vehicle we've got a frightened young woman who did not hit the man, but saw what happened. According to her, another man ran down the sidewalk as the biker slowed for the intersection and shot him. You're going to see to the one who got shot?"

"Yeah, we're heading there now. Did you get his name?"

"No. You might take a look at the female. She's very pale."

"We've only got the two of us. You should call another rig for her." Tavis followed Jasper's lead and slipped into the back to get his bag. Jasper pulled together a monitor and his medic kit and quickly ran to the man on the ground.

"Sir, sir." Jasper tried to wake the patient but got no response. Short of that, he tried to detect a pulse.

"I'm bringing the monitor," Tavis called, and ran up beside the man.

While Tavis checked his vitals, Jasper searched for ID and found it in his back pocket. "Peter, are you with me? I need you to tell me how you feel."

"His pulse is rapid, his pressure is dropping," Tavis reported and prepared to give him saline solution.

Jasper continued to try to raise him while he checked for problems. "He's got road burn on his head, but no apparent contusions." He moved down the body to where blood was staining his pants.

"Oh, oh, oh," the man moaned.

"Don't try to sit up until I get you thoroughly examined. "What is your name?"

His eyes fluttered open. "Pete." His face contorted. "Pete Royal. Geez, my leg hurts."

"What day is it?" Jasper asked.

"Umm," he rubbed his forehead. "Wednesday?"

"That's right." Jasper sat back on his heels and held his hand against the wound.

"Oww! That hurts, man."

"I'm sorry. I need to put pressure on your leg. You're bleeding quite a bit. Try not to move your head until we can get you to the hospital."

Jasper helped Tavis slip the backboard under the man to support him. Then Jasper put one bolster pillow on each side of Pete's head and taped them there to stabilize it.

"Okay, Tavis, on three. One, two," they counted, then lifted Pete onto the stretcher.

"Grab his helmet," Jasper told Tavis.

"We're going to take you to the back of the ambulance so we can do triage," Tavis said, tucking the helmet at the foot of the stretcher.

Inside the rig, Jasper cut open the pants in the area where the bullet tore through. He wrapped it in a pressure bandage. "This will help with the bleeding. I'm going to give you a sedative, so try to relax. We'll be at the ER soon."

Tavis radioed the dispatcher. "This is 2216. We have an urgent patient aboard and we are en route about ten minutes out."

"How are you doing, Pete?" Jasper put his hand on the man's shoulder.

"Not great. But on this medication I don't care so much," he said.

"I guess you got ambushed, that right?"

"I didn't see it coming. I don't know who shot me or why?"

"The police will investigate that. I gave you just enough sedative to relax your nerves. You have to stay awake for a while yet in case of concussion. You just need to stay calm and let the docs in the ER take care of you. We're almost there."

Jasper stayed sitting beside Pete to keep an eye on him, but his thoughts drifted back to Dobson. He couldn't keep her out of his mind, but had to focus on patient care first. Maybe it was time for a real date. One in which he would take her out to dinner at a nice restaurant where they could get seafood or pasta and good wine. Or maybe he could take her on an adventure, like a Saturday at the Dunes Bay Rock'em Wall Climbing place. Or that zip line out at Recreation Park.

Then again, maybe something quiet and beautiful. Yeah, then dinner. That would be different.

Tavis pulled into the ER and Jasper threw open the back doors and picked up the stretcher under Pete's head while Tavis lifted his feet.

"We're here, Pete. We're going to hand you over to the doctors and nurses. Pete?"

Pete didn't respond.

Jasper and Tavis rolled the stretcher into the ER.

"This is Pete Royal," Jasper recounted to Dr. Smith. "He was awake. He's all yours now."

"Thanks, guys." Dr. Hannah Smith and a nurse transferred him to a bed, and Jasper and Tavis were back in the rig, ready for the next call.

Jasper sat in the passenger seat and leaned his head against the window. It had been a simple call but with some mystery. He wouldn't be surprised if it turned out that Pete lied about not knowing who shot him. Relief that the call hadn't turned out worse outweighed his curiosity, because there was always a chance that the next call could be traumatic.

His throat closed at the thought. Fear of his job was growing. Was quitting the only way out?

CHAPTER 20

The scent of good coffee and fries wafted over Dobson when she walked through the door at Darcy's Dinner. Too bad she wasn't at all hungry.

She scanned the dining room for Wynne. She didn't see him anywhere, but Tricia walked up to her.

"Want a table or booth? Is Jasper going to be joining you?" Tricia asked.

Hands on her waist made her shiver.

"A booth please. No Jasper. This girl is with me." Wynne's voice sliced through her like ice.

"Oh, my bad. Is that right, Dobson?" Tricia gave her a pointed gaze.

She brushed his hands off her, close to regretting agreeing to this meeting. "It is," she said, trying to keep the quiver out of her voice.

She followed Tricia to the booth, feeling Wynne's presence behind her. She could do this. She could manage the situation and be strong.

She slid into the booth, confidence solidifying.

Wynne slid in close to her side. "Isn't this nice," he stated. "Just like old times." Cynicism dripped from his words.

Tricia stood beside the booth, eyeing Wynne up and down. "The menu is on the wall. I'll give you a little time to decide. Yeah, that will be so nice." She turned to walk away and furrowed her brow at Dobson.

"Oh, we're not having lunch, just coffee for me," she said.

"I'll have coffee too," he said, smiling up at Tricia.

Dobson stared into Wynne's eyes and jumped in. "What brings you to Dunes Bay?"

"You know why I'm here. I wanted to see you. I want to know what you intend to do about us." He leaned closer to her. "You slipped out of town without a word to me. After all we meant to each other, you hurt me."

"I'm sorry, but tell me about your wife. How is she doing?" It felt good to challenge him.

He cringed and smirked. "We're back to that."

"We never left *that*." She scowled, angry that he dared to blame her for his problems.

"She doesn't have anything to do with our encounters." He reached for her hand but she pulled back. "What do you want me to say?"

"I'm doing important work here. All I want is to be left alone." She looked straight into his eyes and was not surprised to see fire. She dismissed his anger and went on. "What do you want?"

His eyes narrowed. "Pay back."

Again, not surprised. "Pay back for what?"

"For causing Bryan Merdoch's suicide and ruining my marriage. You really fucked up my life, you know."

"I can't change what happened. It makes me sad that Bryan turned to crime. It makes me sadder that you did too. Hah," she scoffed. "You think I owe you something for, quote, ruining your life? Think about what you did to me."

"What do you mean?" he leaned against the back of the seat and smirked.

"It doesn't matter," she said. "But know this, I did not get away from you and the Chicago PD soon enough."

"You don't get to just walk away. You were disloyal to the blue and I'm going to do all I can to put you in your place. Whatever it takes to make you feel pain, just as I have."

"Excuse me. Dobson, is everything all right?" It was Tricia.

Dobson took a long breath and filled with gratitude. "Thank you. I'm fine."

Tricia stared again at Wynne. "You okay, sir? You look a bit hot under the collar."

"No problems here." He smiled a sick little smile. "We're just catching up. Did you know Dobson used to work in Chicago? And did you know she left the department in chaos when she moved to Dunes Bay?"

Tricia leaned on the table top. "Nope. All I know is she's my friend and the diner doesn't put up with people like you who put their nose in places they have no business."

"No business, no business. I have every right to be here and enjoy a cup of coffee with a former girlfriend."

Dobson shrunk inside to the word "girlfriend." "Yes, that's right. I'm a former girlfriend. I could say a lot of hurtful things to you about that. Instead, couldn't we just admit we had great sex and a little fun… until I discovered you had a wife? Let's just be done with it all."

Glee at being herself and saying what she wanted to say filled her. And the surprise on Wynne's face was the icing on the cake.

"Huh. That was well put. Very clear." Tricia spun and walked away with a smile on her face.

"I don't like your tone." Wynne spit out the words. "I lost my job, my wife, and a friend. And you get a brand spanking new job and apparently a new boyfriend, from what I've seen. It's not right."

"Then tell me what it would take to make it right. I've left my home town, worked hard for what I've accomplished, and had a lot of setbacks. Isn't that enough?"

"I'll let you know," Wynne said, and walked out of the diner.

Tricia walked up and slipped into the booth opposite Dobson. "Is everything all right?"

Dobson's shoulders drooped. "I don't know. Give me some time and I'll let you know."

"Was that creep a friend of yours? He stormed out of her like he was angry," Tricia said.

"He used to be a friend, a lying, cheating friend. I walked away from his toxicity and he is mad about it. Oh well. I don't miss him and I want him out of my life entirely. I didn't know he'd found me in Dunes Bay until this morning."

"Let me guess, he's threatening you with something. Can I help?" Tricia fiddled with the napkin holder.

"I can handle him. I can deal with him. It's what he might do to other people in Dunes Bay that concerns me." Tricia's offer to help touched her heart, but Dobson was alone in this mess that she brought down on herself.

Tricia stood up beside the booth and eyed Dobson. "Is it Jasper you're afraid might get hurt?"

"He is one person, yes. And you. He didn't like your tone, remember?"

"Please, don't hesitate to ask for help. You have people here who care about you." Tricia walked back to the kitchen, leaving Dobson to think. It was true that Wynne had a temper. If Wynne hurt anyone, he could be arrested. But she'd rather find a way to get him out of town before anyone got hurt.

"Oh crap," she exclaimed remembering she had an important task to take care of before she could do something about Wynne. Her other source of danger to her friends and her mother needed to be addressed.

She hurried to her office and sat down to make a call. "Hey Zachary, this is Dobson. I need you to arrest Robby Ricci. I'm sending you the paperwork right now. I need him to go in a cell today. He is one of the men who threatened my mother."

"I can put somebody on that. I'll contact you when it's done. Is everything going well?" Zachary asked.

"I need to continue pressuring Teddy. Robby is his nephew so that should show Teddy I mean business. Cooperate or see all his family members in jail."

"I see. You've got a plan." Zachary chuckled.

I'm juggling a few things and crossing my fingers all the balls will come together neat and tidy. Wish me luck?"

"You bet. Just be careful. The Espositos don't mess around. With Marco, Franco, and Robby in jail, that will make at least three of their top men put away. You're stirring up a hornets nest, Dobson."

"That's exactly what I'm trying to do."

"I trust that you know what you're doing, just stay aware," Zachary urged.

Exhilaration filled her as she hung up the phone. Her plan was in play. Soon she would give Teddy another poke to cooperate with her investigation. That meant she was another step closer to extending Teddy's sentence.

* * *

JASPER CHECKED HIS WATCH. It was four o'clock, just two more hours and his shift would be over. He resumed organizing the ambulance triage area.

Fortunately, it didn't require much attention to go through that mundane task. His thoughts were on Dobson and how he could see her this evening. He stuffed his cell phone into the pocket of his uniform and walked out of the building at a brisk pace. He crossed the courtyard, his eyes searching for Dobson, and entered the police department building.

"Hey Hector, how are you doing?"

"Jasper, my man. Things are good. What's up?" Hector asked.

"I'm looking for Dobson. Can I walk back to her office?"

"Sure. You know the way?"

"Yup, thanks!"

He wound his way to her office and lit up when he saw her through the glass window. The door was open, so he stuck his head in. "Knock knock?" he said.

"Jasper," she said, a lilt in her voice. "Come in. Boy it was tempting to answer, Who's there?"

"You should have. I like a good knock, knock joke."

Her office was how he'd imagined it: Full bookshelves, stacks of files on her desk, and a small moon sculpture on the corner of her desk. He stepped up behind her and placed his hands on her shoulders. "Need a massage," he asked, and started squeezing her neck.

"Mmm, that feels great." Dobson closed her eyes and leaned into his hands.

"Your muscles are very tight. I should work on you sometime." He stepped around her desk and smiled. "I just wanted to see you and I have a moment, so I thought I'd drop in."

"Thanks. You didn't ever startle me because I know your touch," she said, beaming. "Sorry, I've got to go. Police business."

"It was nice to see you for a minute," he said. "Would you come over tonight? Have dinner and hang out? Just the two of us."

"Sounds marvelous. I'll check in on my mom and text you. What time?"

"I get off at six, so any time after that. I'll get pizza."

"Okay."

He wanted to linger, kiss her, hold her in his arms, but instead he walked out the door and out into the sunshine. It was bright, nearly blinding. He thought of his sunglasses sitting in the rig. But the walk across to the fire station was brief.

"Don't turn around and don't talk."

Jasper didn't recognize the voice but he was acutely aware that a gun was shoved into his back.

CHAPTER 21

The list of people Dobson had to call was getting longer and longer, which was good. The case was narrowing down, requiring her action on several fronts. She unwrapped the sandwich she'd picked up on her way back to the office and took a bite and perused the call list. To start with, she called her mom. Her mom had a cell but she always answered the landline. They must have been the last people in the world to own a landline, she mused.

"Hello," her mother answered.

"Mom, how are things there? Is everything quiet?"

"Yes. I just looked out the windows and the officers are out there. In the hot sun. I feel bad. I may take them some lemonade."

"You don't have to do that, Mom. Just stay inside and be safe."

"I hear you, sweetie."

"That sounds noncommittal. I can't stress enough the need for you to stay inside."

"Okay, I will." Cecilia's voice was perky, which drew concern in Dobson.

"I'm coming home after work, but I'm going for dinner at Jasper's house if you don't mind." Dobson shoved a pile of files to the other side of her desk. The piles were closing her in.

"How lovely. I'll be fine."

"You can think about it. Jasper won't mind if I pass." Excitement and anxiety mixed insider her, wanting time alone with Jasper and to protect her mother.

"Don't be silly. You should go, have fun." Cecilia chuckled. "You must feel cooped up at home tending to your mother. I would feel better knowing you're having a little bit of fun."

"Okay. I'll see you later. Take it easy."

Dobson pursed her lips, thoughtful. She was walking a tightrope between work and home, worried her mother would fall off and disappear forever. But enthusiasm for an evening with Jasper bounced in her chest, making it hard to focus on work.

Next up, Soren Lucia. She punched in the phone number she'd gotten from the FBI and tapped her pen on the desk while the phone rang. Once, twice, three times, four, five, six. About ready to hang up, she stopped when she heard a man answer.

"Hello?"

"Hello, Mr. Lucia this is Detective Ramirez from the Dunes Bay Police Department. I'd like to talk with you for a minute."

"What do you want?" he growled. "I haven't done anything wrong."

"I'm looking for information, that's all."

"Okay, what do you want?" She heard him blow out, which meant he smoked. She picked up an evidence bag and stared at the butt of a cigarette inside it.

"I'll be blunt. I'm looking for information regarding a recent murder. Could you—"

"Whoa, whoa. I haven't murdered anybody. Why you calling me?"

"Hold on. I'm not interested in you for the crime. I want to know if someone demanded you do something to Devin Raye. Do you know him?"

Dobson heard him breathing on the other end, but he didn't respond.

"Mr. Lucia? Did you get instructions to kill Mr. Raye? That's all I'm asking you. If you can tell me if that happened to you, I can possibly protect you." Dobson's heart pounded hard.

"I told you. I didn't kill anyone. I'm not saying I didn't rough him up. That's what Teddy told me to do. So how would you protect me?" Soren's voice quivered a little.

"Mr. Lucia, I have evidence you were at the scene of the crime. But if you cooperate, I can offer you immunity from prosecution. I would also protect you from the Esposito crime family with entry into the government's Witness Protection Program."

"What makes you think I know the Espositos? I don't have anything to do with them." He coughed hard.

She waited for him to stop coughing and allowed him time to gather his thoughts.

A long minute passed.

"Um, how do I know you won't go back on your promise? How do I know you're not lying to me?"

"You don't know. Let me be clear. I don't want you. I want Teddy Esposito. If you can help me connect him to Devin's death—"

"He died? I saw an ambulance take him away. When did he die?" Soren's voice rose an octave.

"He didn't die at first. He died in the hospital a couple days later. You didn't know that?" She had to go slow but it was driving her nuts.

"No. I just beat him up pretty bad. That's what Teddy asked me to do. More like told me to do it or else, because Devin was skimming money from the Espositos. But I did not shoot Devin."

"So you can connect Teddy, under oath, with Devin's beating. Is that right?"

"Yes, if you can protect me. If you can't, it won't matter what I do, Teddy will kill me."

"Frankly, I'm surprised you're still alive. I would like you to come to the police department so we can talk details and get you protected right away. I'm going to talk to someone who can tell me exactly what I need to do to protect you.

"What? You don't have any authority to protect me!? Oh, man," he moaned.

"I didn't say that. But you must understand you would be held accountable for your crimes were you to break the rules of an agreement."

"I swear on my mother's Bible I will not fraternize with the Esposito family or any other criminal," he vowed. "I have been low on the totem pole in the organization so in addition to handling potential clients, I've run drugs and assisted in money laundering. I just want to be up front."

"That's good, Soren. You're doing the right thing and I appreciate the steps you're taking." Dobson meant what she said. His testimony would make a difference in her case against Teddy.

He let out a long sigh. "So, how does this work?"

"You come into my office and we'll talk. How soon can you get here?" The sooner the better. And hopefully before Teddy has Soren killed.

"I'll be there in twenty minutes."

Dobson prepared her questions while waiting, but she was ready to interrogate Soren. She'd been waiting for a long time for an opportunity to talk with someone in the inside who could tell her Teddy's role in Devin's death.

She got a cup of coffee from the coffee pot and walked back to her desk. Urgency swept through her. She'd been close to this moment several times during her investigation. Eagerness to secure Soren's testimony trembled inside her.

She sipped the office coffee, startled by its robust flavor. Maybe Weirling was right. The coffee wasn't too bad. But it was no Coffee Easy coffee.

The receptionist walked up to Dobson's, smiling and giggling. "Dobson, there is a Soren Lucia here to see you. He's waiting at the front desk. He's a looker. Tall, dark, and handsome." She giggled again.

"I've never met him. He's here on business. Could you bring him to the interview room?

The receptionist's expression sobered. "Of course."

Dobson waited a couple minutes before joining Soren, just to let him sit with his tension. She expected a lot from him and wanted him nervous.

She continued to drink coffee while reviewing her questions. After a bit she checked the clock. It was time.

Dobson headed down the hall to the first interview room and sat down at the other side of the table from Soren. He jiggled one of his legs and stared at her.

"Thanks for coming in, Soren. If you cooperate, this won't take long. Would you like a cup of coffee?"

"Yeah, sure. Can I get cream and sugar in it?"

"Of course." Dobson stuck her head out the door and hollered to Tandy. "Could you please bring a cup of coffee, some sugar, and the creamer?"

"I'll be right there," she said.

"Why don't we get started. She pushed a button on the camera sitting in the room. "Your testimony will be recorded."

"I don't want to recorded," Soren complained.

"It's just procedure," she said. "It makes everything so much easier all the way around. It's not going to be used against you," she tried to reassure him. "If anything, it's an assurance that nothing inaccurate will be credited to you."

"Okay, as long as you're not lying to me. How do I know you're not lying to me?"

"You don't. Any more than I can be sure you're not lying to me."

"You got me there." Soren grinned and squinted his eyes.

She turned her attention to her questions. "What was your relationship with Devin Ray?"

Soren slumped in his chair. "I had no relationship, per se. But he was an acquaintance I met in the Esposito family organization."

"How long have you been a member of the Esposito organization?" She kept her gaze tight on Soren, looking for signs of lying.

"I was recruited into the organization two years ago. Teddy's brother Marco approached me when I was showing him a property he wanted to develop."

"Why did he approach you?"

"I don't know. Do bears like honey?"

"Please try to stay relevant," she said sternly. Inside she was laughing at his colloquial use of the language.

"What I'm saying is I work as a successful real estate developer and he wanted to bring what I offered to the organization. He told me I could make a lot more money working in conjunction with his company. It sounded good."

"Okay, so you've been working to help the Espositos expand their holdings and providing money laundering opportunities, right?"

Soren sat erect and pounded his fist on the table. "You said you weren't interested in me, so why all these questions about me and my work?"

She restrained her frustration with him and smiled. "It's standard procedure. Don't worry. Just answer the question."

"Could you repeat it?"

"Sure. Could you summarize your role in the Esposito's organization?"

"I sell property. I introduce certain clients of mine to Marco and Teddy and I launder money for the organization." He raised his eyes to look at the ceiling. "I'd say I've been working in that capacity for two years."

"And did things change recently for you?"

Soren rubbed his chin and frowned. "Ah, yeah. I was told the organization needed me step up into a greater capacity."

"What did that involve?"

Soren stared at her for a minute. "Teddy himself asked me to mess up Devin Raye."

"Clarify. What did it mean to you to mess up Devin?" She pinned his gaze.

"Um, well. It meant to beat him up pretty bad."

"And did you?"

"I did. Teddy requires unflinching obedience. He said I had one chance to do the job or he would send Marco and Franco to beat me up." He dropped his stare to the floor. "Teddy had old police reports on me for assault, so I guess he thought I was the right guy. I didn't want to do it, but a beating from his guys is serious business."

"Why didn't you report Teddy to the police for what he asked you to do?"

"Because I'm not stupid. And I'm not a rat. He doesn't accept no for an answer and he despises being ratted out. If I did anything sneaky, he'd find out. He knows all the right people and where their bodies are buried."

"How did you know that?" Soren was cooperating and presenting information with forthrightness. He was still jiggling his leg and sat with tight shoulders, all signs of duress.

"He made that very clear and I believed him. I've heard things that proved he was telling the truth. So I followed Devin out to the country and rammed him off the road. He tried to get out of the car and started fighting with me. After I'd knocked him out, Teddy showed up. He ordered me to keep it to myself and leave. He said he would take care of clean up. I actually drove around the corner a ways and hiked back. I hid at the top of a hill behind some bushes. I just wanted to see what Devin would do when he woke up."

He sat quietly for a couple minutes.

"Go on," Dobson said.

"I saw Teddy shoot Devin in the head."

"Could you confirm Devin's death before you left?" Her heart beat hard. These were details Soren couldn't know unless he was there.

"No, I did not. I scrambled to get out of there."

Hours later, Dobson left work and stopped in at home to check on her mother. She set her up with a prepared chicken and vegetable casserole she could bake and was on her way to Jasper's house. She heaved a sigh and let her shoulders relax in her car. She didn't have Teddy wrapped up yet, but it was simply a matter of time. In discussion with Zachary about what she'd learned from Soren, her case advanced much closer to prosecution. He assured her agents would have Teddy in jail by morning the next day.

She pulled into Jasper's driveway and turned off the ignition, taking a minute to check her face. She smiled at herself. She'd done it.

She'd invested in her knowledge and skill and blooming confidence to put Marco and Franco in jail for possession and distribution of meth, and pinned a murder on Teddy. He wouldn't be leaving prison for a long time.

Her mother was set up with dinner and a movie with guards protecting her and now Dobson walked up Jasper's backstairs for an evening with him. Jasper had been right. She had it in her to triumph over false beliefs and fear. Good things could happen to her.

She knocked on the back door and waited to see Jasper's smiling face.

Finally, Jasper opened the door. Dobson sucked in a breath.

"What's going on here? Jasper, oh Jasper," she exclaimed.

Cuffs on Jasper's hands scared her. Duct tape across his mouth made her heart stutter. She raced through the door, her gun raised, and found Wynne at Jasper's back pointing a gun at him.

"Now don't get all riled up, or I might just shoot this thing," Wynne warned with his gun. "Put your gun down. I saw you with Jasper on the beach the other night. You expect you can just go on with your life with him, the new boyfriend, and a life while I'm tossed aside and jobless? No. I won't have it. I want payback for what you've done to me. I want you to suffer."

A shiver sliced through her, realizing Wynne meant to kill Jasper. She eyed Jasper. His eyes pleaded with her to drop her gun, but she shook him off. Still aiming her gun at Wynne, she swiftly kicked the gun out of his hand and dove for it before he could get to it. "Now that I have both guns, get down on your knees with your hands above your head.

"No," Wynne said, lifting his chin. "What are going to do, shoot me? You won't shoot me. You know that and I know—"

Before he could finish his sentence she shot him in the shoulder and he dropped to the floor. "I guess you were wrong. I knew I would shoot you."

"You shot me," Wynne bellowed.

"I did. Now shut up," she demanded. She called Hector for backup and EMS.

She turned to Jasper, who had slipped out of the cuffs and torn off the tape. "Here," he said, and tossed her the cuffs.

She caught them and swiftly put them on Wynne.

"You shot me, you bitch," Wynne repeated.

Dobson ignored him "How did you get the cuffs off?" she asked Jasper.

"It's an old trick I learned from a friend in the police department. I'll tell you about it later." Jasper grinned at her through a bruise on his cheek. "That was good maneuvering, by the way."

"Thanks! I've been practicing my moves."

"I've seen your moves and they're spectacular," Jasper teased.

"I need to go to the hospital." Wynne said. "I'm bleeding!"

"Don't worry. It's only a flesh wound," Dobson assured him. "An ambulance is on its way. I'm surprised you're so upset. You're a cop, or I mean, ex-cop. You know procedure. I guess you're not as strong as you thought."

Jasper wrapped his arms around Dobson and pulled her close. "I want to see more of your moves," he whispered in her ear.

She savored his warmth. It helped bring heat back to her skin. "I suppose that could be arranged," she said, while keeping an eye on Wynne.

Sirens sounded in the distance, telling her help was near. Jasper stood above Wynne, watching him. "Don't do any funny business. The cops are here."

"I can't do anything. I'm shot."

"Good. Maybe that will teach you to listen when Dobson says leave her alone." He nudged at Wynne's leg with his foot.

The siren's sounded outside, then went quiet, as the EMTs nodded at Jasper and plowed through the door right behind the officers.

"Dobson, it looks like you've got the suspect under control," said her fellow officer, Jordan.

Wynne lifted his head. "She shot me."

"I did. He threatened me and Jasper with a gun."

Jordan read Wynne his rights and the EMTs walked him out to the rig.

"Be careful," Wynne directed. "I'm hurt pretty bad. I need pain meds."

"We'll bandage your wound and check you out, but it looks like Dobson just winged you," said one of the EMTs. "You're going to be fine."

Dobson and Jasper followed them outside and found Hector leaning against a cruiser.

"Hector, why are you standing out here?" she asked.

"I have a message for you, Dobson. It's from Teddy."

Icy slivers cut through her. "What? From Teddy Esposito?"

"The very," he said. "He called me, on what we determined was a burner phone, at the department and said to tell you your mother is fine. For now."

CHAPTER 22

Thoughts ran in circles in her head, round and round like a tiger chasing a monkey. She balled her fists. "No, no, no!" she hollered. "Do you think it's true?"

Hector rolled his shoulders. "I'm afraid I do. Teddy escaped last night from prison, with help from a guard."

"A prison guard helped him how?" she asked.

"What's been figured out is the guard summoned him to the laundry room and hid him in there. Then when the laundry truck came to make a pick up, they rolled out Teddy in the laundry cart. After that, we don't know where he went."

"So Teddy picked up my mom?" She was getting overwhelmed, it all seemed so farfetched.

"Actually, the officers keeping watch were inside your condo. It appears your mother had invited them in for lemonade. Someone broke in and knocked out the officers. Your mom was not there when I went over to check on her after I got the message from Teddy." Hector put his hand on Dobson's shoulder. "I'm so sorry this happened. We're looking for Teddy and your mom as we speak, and touching base with all known associates." He cleared his throat. "To be sure, the officers should not have gone inside. They will be reprimanded." He stared at her without saying anything.

"Have you told me everything?" It looked like Hector was holding back, by the grim look on his face.

"There is more to the message. Teddy demanded you drop the investigation."

"Or?" She barely spoke.

"I think you know what?"

"Mom will disappear forever." Her voice caught in her throat.

Processing what she just learned, Dobson froze. How could she make this right? She gritted her teeth, thinking of Teddy. How dare he?

"How can I help?" Jasper asked.

She knew better than to crumple in his arms. She had to be strong and find her mother. Then she'd go after Teddy and his minions, no holds barred.

She touched Jasper's face. "You can go inside and stay safe."

"Come with me. We can figure this out. I know we can." Jasper's words were urgent, insistent. "The Espositos aren't after your mom, they want you. You need to get out of sight and gather your thoughts before they find you."

He had a point. This was all different having someone she could trust and work with. Old insecurities admonished her to stay away from outside help.

But things were changing. She knew that now. "Okay, let's go inside," she said. "Hector please stay in touch. You can reach me on my cell."

"You stay in touch with me, Dobson," he insisted. "You're not in this alone."

"What did you say?" she asked.

"You have people you can rely on." He gave her an encouraging smile and climbed in his cruiser.

. . .

INSIDE JASPER'S HOUSE, he made coffee while Dobson dropped her things on the coffee table in the living room and sank into the couch. She looked beat, and he wanted so much to solve her problems. What did Gray say? I can't solve other people's problems, it's not my job. But I can believe in them and that they'll solve them themselves.

"I know you," he said. "You brought your laptop with you, didn't you?"

"It's right there in my bag. Why?"

"As you know, this isn't the first time the Espositos have kidnapped a family member, it just happens to be your family that is affected this time." Jasper pulled memories from a few months ago. "In the thick of things with Emma and Adrian Moss, before they turned witnesses, Rachel hired Rhys to search for evidence in her parents' law firm computer files to prove they were or were not still involved with the mob as they had been."

"Yes, I know that about the case." Dobson knitted her brow. "What are you getting at?"

"Rachel uncovered a list of the companies the Esposito's organization had laundering money for them. The file was under Acorn Financials, if I remember correctly. If you can access that file, we could sort out possible places where they've taken your mother."

"So, you want me to hack into Moss Attorneys at Law's computer system and locate the list, right?" Dobson's eyes were wide. "And then we'll check out all local companies on that list."

'Right. You sound dubious. It's just a thought. My brothers will help."

Her eyes got wider. "I'm not going to ask them to put their lives in jeopardy like that."

"You don't have to ask. They'll do it. I'll do it." Jasper watched her eyes shoot daggers.

Dobson jumped to her feet. "I don't want you sticking your neck out. I think I love you, Jasper. More and more." Tears crept down her cheeks.

In an instant, he shot to her side. "Sweetheart, I appreciate that. I don't want to die. But sacrificing for someone you care about is loving. If I had my way, you'd stay at the police department until all this mess is over."

"I'm not doing that. I'm not sitting this one out," she stated. She shook her head. "Okay, but let's go to the sisters' law firm and ask them if they can access the list," she exclaimed.

"That is a better plan. Let's go," Jasper said, and led her outside. "I'll drive my car." He stopped in his track. "Okay?"

"I'll just follow." She opened the driver's door.

JASPER WALKED inside the modest building where the sisters' office was located and found the Steele and Moss office down the hall.

It was after hours, but the front door was unlocked. They headed through the reception area and down a hall.

"Rachel, Cherish," Jasper called. Seconds later, both came out of their individual offices, beaming.

In turn, they wrapped Jasper in a hug and offered a handshake to Dobson.

"To what do we owe this pleasant surprise?" Cherish gushed.

"We have a favor to ask," Jasper started. "But let me first say, you've done some superior decorating with your office."

"Thank you," Cherish said.

"It's a work in progress," Rachel added.

Dobson nodded. "I agree with Jasper. It's simple, sleek, and professional."

"We love it, and are excited about being able to make decisions about what we want to do for clients here, away from our dad and mom," Rachel said.

"Was that a hard decision to make?" Jasper asked. "There's been so much going on lately that I haven't heard any family discussion about your new firm."

"There were some hurt feelings, but Rachel and I knew we had to break away. Mom and Dad are still processing our move," Cherish said. "It's only been a month or two since we opened our practice."

"Good luck to you both." Dobson twisted her fingers, nervous to ask for a favor. "So, we need your help. We expect to pay your fee for a consultation."

Rachel dismissed the thought with a wave. "Don't be ridiculous. You're family. We don't charge family."

Jasper followed the sisters with Dobson to a conference room.

"Have a seat, both of you," Cherish said, gesturing to the chairs at the table.

Rachel poured water in glasses from a pitcher and took a seat. "What's on your minds?"

Jasper made it clear they were together on a plan of action but what was needed was help regarding Dobson's case.

Both of them sat listening to Dobson explain what she needed and why, with no interrupting.

Rachel cleared her throat when Dobson stopped. "My first question is, why are you here Jasper? This is Dobson's case. Are you and your brothers planning to step in physically speaking if there is danger?"

Jasper pursed his lips. He'd been watching Dobson articulate her request and feeling so proud of her, how could he explain this one?

"Honestly, I'm just here because in addition to her missing mother, a couple of hours ago a former boyfriend of Dobson attacked me and threatened to kill me, among other things. I didn't want to leave her alone."

"That's awful!" Cherish said. "Is everything squared away with that now?"

"Yes," Dobson said. "He's been arrested for assault, reckless use of a lethal weapon, and stalking."

"Geez, what else do you have to deal with, Dobson?" Cherish asked. "I'm so sorry. Of course we'll help you get your mother back in any way we can. We know that list of clients and we'll send it to you as soon as we can. I don't know how much help that will be, though. Fingers crossed."

Outside in the car he contemplated how to best be there for Dobson in the time between now and bringing her mother home. His brain hurt from trying to shield her from danger. How had she been living with it every day for so long? His heart went out to her, and he wanted to hold her.

But more than that, he wanted the best for her. He just hoped he could be in her life somehow, somewhere. And she could have her happy-ever-after that she deserved.

CHAPTER 23

"Do you want me to take you home? Jasper assumed she'd like to be alone in her own place.

"No. I can't go home. Not until Mom is found. It would be too empty." She turned her eyes on him. "Could I go to your place? I know that's asking a lot."

"Of course you can. Are you sure you want to, considering what happened there this afternoon?"

"I'm sure." She dipped her head. "You have a home. It's full of life and love." She looked up. "It's where you are."

Her words were precious, delicate. They deserved to be cradled and cared for. He cupped her face and kissed her gently. Her tears dampened his face. "Let's go."

On the drive to his house Jasper kept his eyes on the road and Dobson behind him. Intermittently he gazed at the landscape passing by. He drew in a deep breath and let it out slowly, letting his body and mind take nourishment from the outcrops of sand among the trees and bushes that spotted the rolling hills along the road.

He arrived at his house and parked in the garage, his thoughts immersed in Dobson and her needs. He held the door for her and she walked directly to the couch and dropped in as though carrying a heavy weight on her shoulders.

"Thank you for this," she murmured. "This isn't the kind of evening we planned. I'm sorry."

"No apologies. What do you need from me? Dinner, entertainment, privacy? Please make yourself at home. The guest bedroom is yours."

"All I need is you, Jasper. Just you. You're the something good I need in my life." Her lips parted slightly.

What was she really saying, he wondered. "I love the sound of that." But it wasn't the time to commit. Not when she was under such duress.

Dobson laid her head on his lap and sighed. "I know I've been difficult to be with, especially during the getting-to-know-each-other part. I hope you can be patient with me."

He caressed her head, loving every feel of her hair, her cheeks, her skin. He bent to place a kiss to her head. Her mesmerizing scent filled him. But caution told him to go slow. "No matter what happens, I will always remember the times we've had together."

She rose to her feet, longing in her eyes. "I want more. No holding back. Just for a while, I don't want to think."

He wrapped his arms around her and shoved her against the wall. Frustration from the day and pent up passion drove him. He kissed her hard, relentless, leaning against her, wanting no distance between them. "Don't be afraid." Her breaths were heavy against his chest.

"I'm not. Not now." Their eyes locked, she pulled his shirt over his head and tossed it to the floor.

Unbridled desire tensed his body. How to show her she was precious to him?

Then he stopped thinking. He ripped off her shirt and cradled her breasts in his hands, kissing her skin. It was warm and inviting. He kissed under her chin, his breath coming fast and hard as he trailed kisses to her breasts.

She removed her underwear and stood naked and beautiful before him. A knowing passed between their gazes and he stripped naked.

Slowly he stretched out on the couch, his breaths coming hard as he stared up at her naked body. He offered his hand and she took it and lay out on top of him.

"I want this to be very conscious. I want to learn every cell in your body and every atom," he whispered. "I love you, Dobson."

"I love you, Jasper," she said, her voice hoarse.

He pulled her on top of him and savored her breasts, licking and kissing them as though they were treasure. His body's every part came alive like this was his first time.

She rolled onto the floor on her back, and he dropped kisses across her belly and intimate places. Wriggling, she pulled him up and he thrusted inside her. His mind exploded with so much love for her, he could hardly contain all the sensations firing his body. He paused briefly for protection while she placed kisses to his body. He returned to the floor and caressed her, then covered her with his body.

She kissed him passionately, and he was lost in her love. His body took over, and they rocked together, thrusting over and over until he could no longer hold back.

"Jasper," she said, "I can't wait."

"Don't," he breathed and felt her throbbing against him at the same time that he let everything go. "Oh god, Dobson."

Dobson cried out as the heights of passion peaked. They clung to each other as they got drowsy. He rested his head on her chest as slowly, slowly, their bodies relaxed against each other. Her beating heart thudded against him, connecting them as one.

After a few minutes passed, Jasper roused enough to shift off her to lie beside her heated body. Her eyes still closed, she snuggled close up under his arm and he pulled the sheet over them.

"Mmm…" she murmured. "I'm going to lie here for the rest of the evening. My legs won't hold me yet." She chuckled. "We make a good team."

"Most decidedly. Haven't I been saying that?"

"Yes. You're right, in every way." Dobson's fingers crept down under the sheet. "You feel so good. I would like more of this in my life."

"You feel exquisite." Shades of reality shifted inside him. It won't last, his brain told him. Don't invest in this moment too much, you'll only get hurt.

"You're quiet. What's up?" She ran her fingers over his lips. "You can tell me."

"There's nothing up. I'm simply savoring our intimacy." It wasn't a lie.

"Okay. I don't know if I can hold this peaceful moment for very long. A different reality is going to surface any minute and drag me down." She raised her lips to his and they kissed softly, reverently.

"I confess. I feel that too," he admitted. "I didn't want to spoil the moment so I didn't tell you." He didn't tell her it was a belief that no one really wanted him. Shame for not being loved crept into his gut. "I don't want to sink into old habits, but it's hard to know the way out of them," he blurted.

"Aww…darling, why didn't you tell me? I'm the same. But maybe we can always be forthright about our feelings and allow expression even if it's painful."

He breathed in and out slowly, regaining his sanity. "You're right. True intimacy."

"The kind a couple would have?" She arched her eyebrows and smiled a sultry smile.

"Exactly that kind of intimacy, only ours would be uncommon and very aware. I could enjoy a lot of that in my life." Jasper paused for a minute, weighing his thoughts. "It's something I've been looking for in a relationship for a long time. Could it be you I've been waiting for?"

"Could it be you I can trust with forever?" She grinned.

He offered her his hand and she responded by grabbing it in her own.

"Are you thinking what I'm thinking?" he asked.

"I hope so. We are committing to be there for each other for as long as it works? Blush crept up into her cheeks, which only endeared her to him more.

"I am. Are you?"

He grabbed her up in his arms and spun in a circle. "I am. And knowing us, we'll each work on our relationship to make it a healthy one."

"Speaking of—"

"I need recovery time," he joked.

She smiled. "I didn't mean that. I was about to say, making love with you was the most intimate and satisfying ever," she exclaimed and sat on top of him in fun. "You touched my soul."

"You touched mine. It was a beautiful and sacred thing," he gushed. "But, my stomach is growling. How about I make dinner and we eat out on the deck?"

"Sure," she truly enjoyed their lovemaking, but now that it was over thoughts of her poor mother brought her back to the difficult reality. "But can we keep this feeling a little longer? I don't want to think about anything." Her expression drooped. "Real life is encroaching."

"We can return to our reality inside these moments any time. But can we eat first?"

She pulled the sheet up over their heads. "No. Snuggling first."

CHAPTER 24

"It's here," Dobson said. Anticipation trilled in her chest.

Jasper flipped the pancakes on the grill. "The list? It's here?"

"Yeah." Dobson sat on a stool at the island in Jasper's kitchen scrolling through the list of clients with the Espositos. "Do you mind if I print it?"

"No, have at it."

She ran upstairs to his bedroom where the printer sat on a desk and waited for the multiple pages to print. When it finished, she ran down stairs with the pages. "Can you help me read through these?" she asked.

"Of course. Let me just put breakfast on the table. We can peruse while we eat."

She narrowed her focus to the list, hoping for a miracle. Hector was working on this Thursday, so she'd called and gotten an update on her mother's situation: No word, no clues. It broke her heart into pieces, but she couldn't spend time crying or falling into a pit. If she spent much time thinking about her poor mother being held captive she'd dissolve. There was no time for that.

"Jasper, these pancakes look scrumptious, but I don't feel like eating. My mother is missing and I don't know where she is or if she's okay. I'm so worried."

"I understand, but we need to eat to keep up our strength."

"You're right," she mumbled, and stabbed at a pancake on her plate.

"Yeah, a body's got to eat."

She heard him but just barely.

Where had Teddy taken her Mom? She ran her finger down the list, noting addresses. Remote, not too close to the location of the prison? Frustration boiled in her head.

"This is hopeless," she muttered.

"If the list doesn't help us we'll find another way to find your mother." Jasper refilled his coffee and hunkered down over the list again.

Gratitude for his help and for who he was glided through her, renewing her faith that the impossible could be done. "I'm not familiar with many of these locations."

"I understand. I'll narrow down the list to only those places located in a circumference around Teddy's headquarters."

Jasper quickly started eliminating locations. "Wait a minute. Do you know any places Teddy frequented before he went to prison?"

"You mean like restaurants, bars, places like that?"

"Yeah. If we narrow down for that, it would be smaller and they would be clients." Dobson readjusted her seat and started over from the top on the first page. Suddenly it dawned on her where he might be holed up. "I think I know where he is likely going to be found. He doesn't like to go out. He may be a big menacing guy, but he's terrified of being killed by someone wanting to make a big move. Or by the FBI. He might be holed up in one of his estates, of which he has many. But, there is one on the opposite side of town from the prison. The location is quite remote."

"Can you find it?"

"You bet. But I better get the FBI involved," she said, and called Zachary.

Jasper paced back and forth across from her, thinking out loud.

"We'll need some kind of guns, ammunition, a first aid kit."

Ten minutes later, Dobson hung up after getting assurances of help from Zachary.

"Zachary is going to bring men with guns and meet us there." She took her gun out of a case in her bag and stuffed it in her back holster.

"Where do I put my gun? I mean, I don't have one." Jasper's heart was beating so fast it felt like an airplane readying to take off.

"You don't need one. You're not going." Dobson got her keys out of her purse and marched to her vehicle, Jasper running behind her.

"You don't mean that, sweetheart. I'm going with," he demanded.

"Not this time. Please stay safe." She looked deeply in his eyes, trying to convince him to stay put. "I couldn't stand it if something happened to you. I'll call or text with an update as soon as I have one. I hope it will be that Mom is with me."

"Okay. I'll just be sitting here by myself worrying about you," he said. "Waiting and worrying. But I understand your point. You don't want me hanging around getting in the way. Please take care of yourself. I don't want to you lose you either."

"Thank you, love." Dobson drove out of the driveway and up the lane.

Before she'd gone out of sight, Jasper had called his brothers and put them on a three-way call. "Hi guys. I have a big problem I need help with immediately."

"What is it?" Rhys asked.

"Yeah, what's going on," Gray chimed in.

He explained everything to his brothers and told them it was urgent. "We can get to the estate before all the FBI guys get organized. We don't have to do anything, nothing dangerous, but we could keep an eye on the place. There are going to be guards, mean guards with guns."

"So this will make it a three-peat, where we Steele brothers help out in a dire situation. Geez, I hate to think of Cecilia being held hostage," Gray said.

"We all do. So let's get this group in action. You two meet at the estate. I'll text you the address," Jasper said. "I'm going to drive a rig. Just in case."

"So we sort of have a plan," Rhys said. "We'll meet at the back edge of the property. Hopefully there are trees we can hide behind."

"Hold on," Gray said. "Are we being stupid? I mean, the FBI probably doesn't need us."

"We're not going to get involved. But if they need our help, we'll be ready." Rhys laughed. "I think it's very smart to ban together and help out Dobson and Cecilia."

"Let's stop wasting time talking and get going," Gray said. "I'm out the door right now."

* * *

JASPER PARKED the rig down the road from Teddy's estate and ran to the field behind his house to meet up with Rhys and Gray.

They crouched down in the weeds and prairie plants and tall grasses.

"This house is huge," Gray said. "What does someone do with all that house?"

"Probably whatever he wants," added Rhys.

"Cecilia could be anywhere in all that square footage," Jasper said. "Let's just sit here until the FBI distracts the guards from this side of the place. We won't be helping Cecilia at all if we get caught."

"No, and I sure don't want to know what Teddy's crew would do with us if we get caught," Rhys spouted.

They saw the FBI vehicles speed past them on their way to Teddy's house. They heard a commotion at the front door and stayed put. Guards at the back of the house ran around to the front while FBI agents corralled them and walked them to FBI vehicles.

"My knees are starting to hurt," Gray whispered.

"I'm wondering about that structure over there," Jasper pointed out. "We should check it."

"Stealthy," Rhys said. "We should be stealthy."

Jasper led his brothers through the tall prairie grasses until they reached a small house. Cobwebs hung around the doors and there were no windows. They slid up to the door. Jasper gave the knob a turn.

"Damn, it's locked," he said looking over his shoulder.

Gray pushed his brothers back a bit. "Let's kick it in. What could go wrong? Everyone is paying attention to the front of the house where the action is."

"Okay," said Rhys. "On three. On three we knock it down. One. Two. Three," he whispered hoarsely.

Jasper lunged and slammed his body against the door, at the same that his brothers kicked at it. The door fell inside in splinters.

"That worked," exclaimed Jasper. He stepped over the broken door inside a small, square, empty room. Windows on two walls were covered with hardboard, so no one could see in or out.

A narrow hallway took them to another locked door. Jasper stopped. "Hey, I hear something." He leaned his head against the door. "It's a woman's voice. It's very quiet. Do you hear it?"

Both his brothers put their ears to the door along with Jasper.

"I hear it too," Gray said. "Do you hear it Rhys?"

"I think it's her," Rhys said. "Teddy must have locked her in here. He might have expected company since he's escaped from prison and kidnapped Cecilia."

"Like the FBI wouldn't check out this building," Jasper said.

"Yeah, they just haven't made it here yet," Gray said. "We need to tell them someone's in here."

Jasper took his phone from his pocket. "I'm going to call Dobson." He punched in her number. It rang on the other end just once.

"Jasper, why are you calling me? I'm in the middle of a search." Dobson's voice was pinched and nervous.

"I know. I have to tell you something. There is a person, possibly a woman, locked inside a room in a building at the back of the property. There are a lot of trees around it and the front door was locked but we got in."

"To put it mildly," teased Rhys, listening in on the conversation.

"Okay, I'll be right there."

"How was she?" asked Rhys.

"She was flustered. But she's strong."

Minutes later, Dobson ran through the entry and stopped beside him.

"Jasper, where is the sound," she asked, abruptly. "The agents are searching Teddy's house for my mom and Teddy, but so far they've found nothing. Wait, what are you guys doing here? And why are you holding bats?"

"We're scouting for you, that's all. We brought our bats just in case we needed protection." Jasper shook his head. "Can we break in this door now?"

"No. I'm going to get an agent. You should get out of here," Dobson said.

She quickly called for agents and they came to the building in rapid time.

"Why are you guys still here?"

"The door!" Jasper shouted.

She shook her finger at him, but told the agents to break in the door.

The inside was dark and cold. Jasper longed to help, to do what he could, but he and his brothers stood back, waiting.

CHAPTER 25

*A*drenalin coursed through Dobson as she raised her gun and headed into the darkness. Instantly, a gun sounded and she ducked. It was Teddy. A dim light shone on his face just enough to let her identify him. His arm was around Cecilia's neck and he dragged her forward, closer to Dobson.

"I'm with the FBI. Drop your gun!" she ordered. "Mom, everything is going to be okay."

"The hell it is," Teddy shouted. "I'm going to walk out of here with this fine young lady and you and your cohorts are going to stand where you are and let me pass." He shoved his gun against Cecilia's head. "Otherwise, she's going down first."

Terror sweeping through her tightened Dobson's body. Her mind stuttered. What could she do? She had to stop Teddy, right here and now.

But Mom, good god, what about Mom?

She collected her screaming and hysterical parts and knew she had two jobs to do. Unfortunately, stopping Teddy was paramount or his crimes against humanity would continue. It wouldn't end for her or her mother if she didn't stop him.

"I can't do that, Teddy. You're not leaving this place alive unless you come with me." Her voice was steady. She meant business. Her gun aimed at his head. "Release Cecilia and put down your gun."

"You're bluffing."

Sounds outside of agents gathering up Teddy's people hardened her resolve and gave her hope.

"You really want to die today? I can oblige you." She pulled back the trigger and it clicked impressively.

"Wait!" he cried.

"Wait for what? For you to nerve up and shoot me? I don't think so."

"You won't shoot me. If you really wanted to shoot me you would have done it already," Teddy said.

The sound of Dobson's gun going off startled him and he jumped. "Wait a minute!" he yelled, as parts of the ceiling rained on him from where she'd shot it.

"Mom, kick him, hard!"

Cecilia kicked backwards at his groin and he collapsed.

"Come on, Mom. Over here. I've got you covered." The scene before her slowed down and everything happened as though in slow motion. "Run Mom!"

Teddy rolled on the floor, hollering while Dobson ran to her mother and wrapped her arms around her.

"Jasper, take mom outside!"

Jasper took Cecilia's hand. "Let's go," he said to Gray and Rhys, then led her out of the building.

An agent brushed past him on his way out. Another one ran in the room, gun pointed. "FBI. Freeze, Teddy."

With three guns aimed at him, Teddy stilled.

Dobson ran to him, cuffed him, and pulled him to his feet. "You're under arrest." She read him his rights as she escorted him out of the building, with the two agents guarding from behind.

Outside, the area was quiet, ominous. She tapped down the fear slithering through her. Nothing would stop her now. She waved away the agents. This was between her and Teddy.

"Here's your way out," she said, pointing to one of the parked vehicles.

Suddenly he rammed his head against hers. It stunned her and she stumbled backwards and fell to the ground. She watched him run toward another vehicle as one of his men popped out from behind a line of trees. The man brandished a gun. "Freeze or I'll gun you down right here," he yelled.

At the car, another man helped Teddy into a van and they sped off.

Instantly, Dobson got to her feet and looked around for an agent.

"Keys, I need keys," she yelled, taking off toward another vehicle. Jasper jumped in front of her grabbing her arm.

"We can take my bus. The guys are already in it. I have an advantage driving an ambulance." He handed Cecilia over to one of the agents. "Please take her home and make sure guards are in place."

Swiftly, they all ran to the ambulance and climbed in. Jasper took off after the vehicle Teddy was in, horns blaring and siren screaming.

"You need to floor it," Rhys said.

"Don't you think he knows what he's doing?" Gray asked. "He drives this thing all the time, at a fast rate of speed. Leave him alone. He's a professional."

"All right, all right." Rhys settled back against the seat in the back of the ambulance. "He knows I respect him."

"Can you two quiet down?" Jasper asked. "And for the record, you don't respect me. Never have."

"What?" Rhys and Gray said at one time. "We've always respected you, little brother. You're the one we admire for your laid back attitude and friendliness."

"I would never know it. I've felt like the ugly step-child for a long time. Don't get me wrong. You guys are great. Too great. It's a lot to live up to. And the way you treat me makes me feel so much less than you two."

"Jasper," said Dobson. "Are you seriously having a heart to heart right now? While we're chasing a very bad man? Shouldn't you focus?"

"I am focused. I can do more than one thing at a time." He chuckled. "Maybe I didn't think it through." He swerved between lanes, passing vehicles on the left, then the right, trying to catch up to Teddy's vehicle.

"You're doing great," Gray said. "We love you to bits, brother. We're just playing around with you. But if you're sincere that we make you feel small, we should stop."

"Have you told Mom and Dad how you feel?" Rhys shifted in his seat as Jasper rounded a corner driving too fast.

"You mean have I told Mom I feel invisible around her? That she takes me for granted? No. I have not."

"Hey, we've caught up to them," Dobson said.

Suddenly, a small truck slammed into the bus, sending the truck directly into Teddy's vehicle. They both were pushed together as they spun as one in the middle of the road, finally coming to rest.

"Are you all okay?" he asked his brothers. "It looks like you've gotten banged up. Sit tight until I deal with Teddy."

"No chance. I'm going with you. I'm fine." Rhys rubbed his head where he'd slammed into the side of the vehicle.

Gray chuckled. "I'm okay. Nothing like a close call to make you grateful you're alive. I'm with you."

"Okay then, let's go." Jasper jumped out of the ambulance and ran with Rhys and Gray to the vehicle Teddy and his goons stole from the agents. He yanked open the door and together they pulled out Teddy and laid him on the ground. He had facial bruises and a small cut was bleeding.

Dobson joined them and cuffed Teddy, while the agents got out of their vehicles and grabbed the other two men trying to run and cuffed them. "Sit down and don't move," one agent ordered. Then he turned to Jasper. "Can you look at these two, also?"

"I will, but first I have to check out Dobson."

He gently brushed her hair off her forehead to check a bruise and a laceration. "A little bump on your head and a cut. I'll fix you right up." He held up one finger. "See my finger?"

"Of course, you silly. I can see fine and I feel fine. I've got to get Teddy secured," she said.

"Hold on. That's a pretty good bang you got. Sit here in the rig for a minute." He pressed a gauze pad to the cut and bandaged it. "An agent got to Teddy before you. He's cuffed along with the others, and waiting to be transported."

"I am a little lightheaded." She looked into his eyes and saw such tenderness she couldn't believe how lucky she was, despite everything that had happened.

Shaken by the crash and Teddy's near escape, Dobson and the Steele brothers stuffed him into one of the FBI's vehicles. "I'll be seeing you soon in court," she said, and slammed the door closed.

"I was worried for a minute, Dobson," Rhys said. "I thought there was no way we could recapture Teddy."

"I was too, but you handled the situation well. Is Teddy going to jail?" Gray asked.

"Once I file my report with confirmation that Teddy ordered Soren to eliminate Devin, he'll go back to prison for a very long time. He won't be my problem anymore."

Glee filled her heart and she turned to find Jasper nearby, talking with the agents and smiling and laughing. It gave her peace to watch him so effortlessly be himself among strangers. In the short time she'd known him he'd become so important to her. Despite the many times he'd told her he wanted her in his life, she was unsure.

When he saw her standing outside, Jasper made a bee line to her.

"Hey, great job," he said. "You saved your mom and took down the infamous crime boss. Congratulations." He leaned close and whispered in her ear. "We can celebrate a little later, okay?"

Her body tingled. "Sounds good."

A few minutes later, DB police drove up, sirens on. Jordan climbed out along with Hector.

"Jasper, did you do this?" Hector asked. He bent down to inspect the damage down to the ambulance.

Dobson rested her hand on one hip. "He did not. It was that truck driver who ran into us, then we rammed into Teddy's vehicle."

"You two okay? And who are those guys leaning against the cruiser?" asked Jordan.

Jasper cleared his throat. "Those are my brothers. I checked everyone and they're fine with just a few bumps and bangs. "

"Okay, that's all we need from you," Hector said, he and Jordan walked to Teddy and his men.

"We were lucky." Jasper ran his arm around Dobson's waist. "That crash could have been bad. Both vehicles were traveling at a high rate speed."

"Yes, you're right." Dobson wanted more, but it wasn't the time or place. "I better get back to the office. Paperwork to do, you know."

"Hey, I was serious about celebrating tonight. I'm going to have everyone over for a celebration dinner. I especially want to see you there, okay?"

Dobson was certain that his eyes didn't purposely look inside her soul, but it happened all the same.

"Yes, I'll be there. Do you want me to bring anything?" she asked.

"No. Just you."

CHAPTER 26

Dobson unlocked her front door and went inside with her mother. She sunk into the couch, exhaustion and relief spiraling through her.

Her mother lowered herself into the cushioned chair she always sat in, and smiled widely at Dobson. "We're safe at home."

"Yes, with one guard at the front and one at the back."

"It was so nice of Jasper to bring us home after I made my statement. He and his brothers are fine young men. His parents are nice too." Cecilia rested her head against the back of the chair.

Dobson watched her relax. Her mother closed her eyes and sighed. Her eyes were slightly sunken, her skin wrinkled a little, but hers was a face Dobson cherished. Her mom had been a complex and strong woman all her life. She worried her lip, thinking about what her mother had been through and what was ahead.

"Mom, would you like some tea?"

"I would. I can get it." Her mother started to rise from the chair but started coughing.

"You can sit. I'll get it."

Dobson heated the water for tea in the microwave and dunked

teabags of green tea and lemon in the cups, then carried them to the living room.

"Thank you, dear."

She sat back on the couch and centered on her mother. "Do you want to talk about your ordeal? We have plenty of time. If it's hard for you, it can wait and maybe you'd like a nap."

"It's too late in the afternoon for me to take a nap. I'd never get to sleep tonight." Cecilia sighed, contentment on her face.

"You might want to anyway. We're invited to a celebration tonight at Jasper's house. If you're not too tired, I'd like you to come."

Her mother's face brightened. "I would like that. I also would like to sit here and just enjoy being with you. Could we do that?"

"Of course. That sounds nice." Dobson sipped her tea, thinking she'd prefer coffee, and settled in. "Can we talk about it?"

"About what?" Cecilia gave Dobson a quizzical look.

"You know."

Cecilia rolled her eyes. "Must we?"

"I feel we should. You told me Gray said he read about a new treatment for lung cancer. Are you considering applying to the study?"

Her mom sighed long and heavy. "I'm uncertain."

Dobson's heart sunk. "Why?" She tried to remain calm.

"I'm stage four lung cancer. My fate is sealed, daughter."

"You don't know that. Besides, this doesn't sound like you. You've overcome so much in your lifetime: racism, immigration, losing Dad. You've been such a fighter."

"Exactly. I'm now tired of fighting. Those fights you mentioned were for something I wanted to fight for myself and for you. This situation is different. I can't win."

The room got quiet and Cecilia closed her eyes. Her breathing was strained, and Dobson's heart hurt. It was after all her mother's choice to make. Whether to hold on to life a little longer or accept death.

She sniffed, tears welling in her eyes. She couldn't. She just couldn't imagine life without her mother.

Her mother sat up straight. "Mija, you are young and full of life.

You've accomplished so many things. I'm satisfied you're going to continue to be okay. You don't need me."

"I do. I'll always need you and want you in my life." Dobson got on her knees in front of her mother and took her hands in her own. "Can you participate in the drug trial for me? You're an important part of my life."

"Can you accept I'm dying?" Her mother's eyes teared up.

"Not without even trying to get more life. Don't you want to stay around and see me get married, have children—your grandchildren—and enjoy picnics in the park together, go to concerts, sit outside and watch my children catch lightning bugs? If you felt better after going through the trial, wouldn't you want to go on living?"

Tears streamed down her mother's cheeks. "You know I do."

"All I'm asking is that you try. We can take things one day at a time. I know it's your decision to make and I will respect whatever you choose. I know I'm being selfish. But you are a good cause."

Her mother's eyes sparkled, just like they used to, and Dobson didn't know if it was because of the tears or if the idea of a longer life sounded good to her.

"Maybe you're right. Maybe I've given up too soon. I may have a little life in me yet." Cecilia squeezed Dobson's hands. "You should have been a lawyer. You can present a good argument."

Dobson threw her arms around her mother. "Thank you, Mom. I'll be with you during the whole process, doing anything I can."

"It will be just the two of us, together."

Dobson held up her little finger. "Pinky swear."

Her mother laughed, and wrapped her finger around Dobson's. "Pinky swear."

"Let's celebrate being together. I want to take you to a coffee shop I think you'll like. Are you up for it?"

"It sounds nice for a change."

"It's called Coffee Easy and it's a short walk away."

* * *

Jasper surveyed the living room and kitchen. Everything looked orderly. He was shooting for comfortable, so he added an afghan his mother made for him to the couch and piled a few books on the end table.

Décor wasn't his forte by far. But making his home welcoming and cozy was what he was all about. With the entire combined family of the Mosses and the Steeles coming over for dinner, he wanted to make everything effortless for them. No thoughts of uncomfortable surroundings would interfere with his guests' good time.

With everyone bringing a dish he didn't have worries about good food for the evening. Dinner at eight meant his company would be arriving soon, so he walked out on the deck and relaxed in one of the chairs. The sky was a soft bright blue with a few early pinks and purples streaking across it.

So much had happened in the six days he'd known Dobson, so much that had changed the tone of his life. Having a relationship with Dobson had proved complicated but it now made a bright and lively spot in his life. Though they'd spoken of commitment, he wasn't sure if it meant they would be exclusive and ongoing into the future.

The issues that had haunted him for too long had shrunk measurably. He knew it was up to him to set boundaries with his family and friends. If his family's expectations of him were overbearing, it was his job to respect himself. If he felt disregarded, he knew it was not due to anything specific his family or friends did, it was his perspective that needed healing. He knew that now.

"Hello, Jasper. Are you home?"

The voice inside his house instantly made him smile. It was Dobson's.

He walked inside and hugged Cecelia. "It's so nice you could make it," he said. He turned to Dobson. "And you, of course." He had eyes only for her. Impatience pushed his nerves to their limit.

"Hi," Dobson said, so casually it grated him. "Come here." She opened her arms and he stepped close. She pulled him closer.

"Finally." He sighed. "I'm glad you're here."

"I'm glad to be here. Maybe we could talk alone sometime while I'm here?" she asked.

He nodded. "I'll make sure we get a chance."

"Jasper, I'd be happy to help out with something. You can put me to work." Cecilia leaned against the kitchen counter.

"Hi all." His mother and father walked in and his mother went straight for Jasper. "Good to see you, son. Where do I put this dish of potato salad?"

His dad gave him a quick pat on his back, a gesture that was so his dad. "Have you and your brothers gone out fishing? Are we eating your catch tonight?" His eyes inspected the dishes sitting on the island.

"Nope. Everyone is bringing a dish, so you'll have to wait and see. "I'm cooking roast beef in barbecue sauce in the slow-cooker."

Dobson picked up the lid to the slow-cooker and sniffed. "It smells yummy."

By dinner time, everyone had arrived. They gathered around the big table on the deck, ready to eat from the many delicious dishes.

Jasper watched as dishes were passed around the table and conversations were lively. That they all could gather in harmony made Jasper's heart happy. If nowhere else, there was harmony right here. His family could weather different opinions, different lifestyles, and difficult situations and still offer love and acceptance to one another.

Dobson cleared her throat and nodded at everyone. "I want to thank every one of you for opening your arms to me and my mother during very tough times and making us feel a part of the family. Thank you. I'll never forget it."

"I'm sorry," Rachel started, "have we not made it clear that once you're one of us, there is no escaping. You and your mother are always a part of this big extended family."

Emma Moss raised her glass of wine. "I'd like to make a toast. But first I want to say, I'm so very sorry for all I've put you through. You all know Adrian and I have done some bad things. We've hurt you and caused a lot of chaos. And, I'm announcing our retirement. It's the right time for us to step away." Emma shared a moment with Adrian.

"We may do a speaking tour discouraging businesses from getting involved with criminal organizations."

"Oh, Mom, Dad. I'm so proud of you," Cherish said.

"But," Emma continued, "through thick and thin, we've all managed to support one another and embrace our differences, or in our case, our crimes. To us!"

"To us," everyone chimed in.

"Raise your glasses again. A toast to our crazy, fun family. Through thick and thin!" Jasper said.

"Through thick and thin," Dobson said, weight from her past lifting off her shoulders. Hope filled her.

Susan Steele stood to make a toast, her glass held high. "I'd like to make an apology to my sons. I've always loved you but I understand that I've let you down. I shouldn't have been so determined you each were happy that I burdened you. I didn't mean to but I know I hurt you. I've leaned on you to make me happy. I'm so sorry for all I've done. And I'm working on making myself happy from here on out."

Susan swiped tears away and raised her glass again. "To you wonderful people. Love love."

"To the wonderful woman who is my mom," Rhys said. "Love love."

The toasts continued around the table, everyone taking a turn to express gratitude.

"I don't know about ya'all, but I'm hungry." Gray said. "All this love is making me hungry. Let's resume eating."

"I hear that," Adrian Moss said through a bite of barbecue beef on a bun.

Conversation continued in a lively manner, filling Jasper's heart. He'd never been so proud of his family. He looked over at Dobson, watching her talk freely and listening to others, just like that. She'd realized who she really was and now shared herself with the others, no more need to raise walls.

He took a moment to enjoy the peace he had and take in the changing sky. The sun was beginning to sink into the horizon and shine like a golden globe lighting up the sky.

He sent a glance in Dobson's direction and she caught it. He motioned toward the beach and she nodded. Jasper didn't say a word of explanation; he simply walked away from the table holding Dobson's hand.

At the beach they kicked off their shoes and stood at the edge of the water, tiny waves washing over their bare feet. Dobson stared at the sky, leaning her head on his shoulder. He draped his arm across her shoulders and stood in awe of Dobson and the nature enveloping them.

"I love you, Dobson," Jasper said and faced her just to see her eyes. "I know we've only just begun to get to know each other. Perhaps it's too soon to tell you, but it's strong in my heart. I know it's enduring." He waited, trying not to anticipate her words.

Her eyes glittered in light from the setting sun. He could survive without her but he didn't want to. He wanted to pour all the love he felt for her into a relationship.

"I don't know what I'd do without you. I can't imagine it. Maybe it's too soon to say, but, Jasper," she paused.

He held his breath for what felt endless.

"I love you more," she breathed. "I can't imagine I'll ever stop." Her face lit up in a glorious smile. "You and your family have wrapped your arms around me and I belong now. I love them almost as much as I love you," she laughed.

He picked her up and they twirled in circles. His heart beat against hers in synchrony and he knew it was a sign of great things to come.

"To us," she said softly.

He bent his head to reach her lips and gently touched them. She moaned and kissed him back hard and passionate.

Jasper matched her passion with his own. "To us."

ACKNOWLEDGMENTS

Thank you to all those who supported me while I wrote this book. All support was helpful, but some I turned to for their expertise. Thank you to my ad hoc proofreader and brainstormer my husband Mike Crandall, who is always ready, willing, and able. Additionally, a big thank you so my best friend and skilled editor HiDee Ekstrom, who rarely missing anything. To my sister Carol Scoot for ready assurance and professional medical input. To my editor Danielle Stockdale at Keen Eye Editing for her patience and amazing editing skills. And for the beautiful cover, I thank Dar Abert of Wicked Smart Designs, who is beautiful in many ways.

ABOUT THE AUTHOR

After cutting her writing teeth as a feature writer for commercial and trade magazines, a reporter for newspapers and radio, and an executive editor for a communications company, bestselling, award-winning author Lynn Crandall tuned her voracious appetite for stories to writing contemporary and paranormal romance, women's fiction, and romantic suspense. In her books, she enjoys taking readers on emotional journeys with relatable characters who refuse to back down, and face challenges and tribulations with heart and soul. She believes every love has a story, and hers is with one handsome husband and a large beautiful circle of family, including her cat Winter. This is Lynn's eighteenth book.

See Me

Writing as Kelynn Storm:
Touch of Breeze